A TIME TO TREASURE

A CHRISTIAN ROMANCE

JULIETTE DUNCAN

D1117104

Cover Design by http://www.StunningBookCovers.com

⌒

Copyright © 2018 Juliette Duncan
All rights reserved.

FOREWORD

HELLO! Thank you for choosing to read this book - I hope you enjoy it! Please note that this story is told from two different points of view – Wendy, an Australian, and Bruce, a cowboy from Texas. Australian spelling and terminology have been used when in Wendy's point of view – they're not typos! As a thank you for reading this book, I'd like to offer you a FREE GIFT. That's right - my FREE novella, "Hank and Sarah - A Love Story" is available exclusively to my newsletter subscribers. go to http://www.julietteduncan.com/subscribe to get the ebook for FREE, and to be notified of future releases.

I hope you enjoy both books! Have a wonderful day!

Juliette

PROLOGUE

"There is a time for everything,
and a season for every activity under the heavens:
a time to be born and a time to die,
a time to plant and a time to uproot,
a time to kill and a time to heal,
a time to tear down and a time to build,
a time to weep and a time to laugh,
a time to mourn and a time to dance,
a time to scatter stones and a time to gather them,
a time to embrace and a time to refrain from embracing,
a time to search and a time to give up,
a time to keep and a time to throw away,
a time to tear and a time to mend,
a time to be silent and a time to speak,
a time to love and a time to hate,
a time for war and a time for peace."

Ecclesiastes 3:1-8

CHAPTER 1

*S*ydney, Australia

Wendy Miller rigidly held her tears in check when her eldest daughter, Natalie, slipped on her beautiful wedding gown. The strapless A-line style suited Natalie's slim figure perfectly, but the prospect of her daughter walking down the aisle without her father brought a massive lump to Wendy's throat.

Wendy's husband, Greg, had suffered a fatal heart attack four years earlier, and although the pain she felt whenever she thought of him had lessened to a dull ache, it was moments like these that brought it rushing back.

"How does it look, Mum?" Natalie stood in front of the full-length mirror, peering over her shoulder at the back of the gown, while Roxanne, the gown's creator, made some minor adjustments.

"It's perfect, sweetheart. You're going to be a gorgeous bride."

Relief filled Natalie's face. "Thank you."

"Your father would have been so proud to walk you down the aisle in this," Wendy added in a wistful tone.

"Mum! You need to stop saying that. It's hard enough as it is."

Wendy bit her lip. Natalie was right. They were both struggling, and Natalie didn't need constant reminders that her father wouldn't be there on her special day when it no doubt was on her mind anyway. Wendy reached out and rubbed Natalie's arm. "I know, sweetheart, I'm sorry."

Natalie stood completely still while Roxanne inspected the gown, making the odd adjustment here and there. Dressed in an oversized multi-coloured loose-fitting shirt, purple tights and yellow sneakers, the young woman didn't look like one of Sydney's top fashion designers, but Roxanne Alexander was a multi-award winner eagerly sought after by the well-to-do, and they'd been fortunate to engage her services. "I won't do the final adjustments until the week before the wedding, but other than that, I think it's done," Roxanne said as she straightened.

Natalie beamed. "I love it so much. Thank you. Now all I have to do is eat salad for the next three months."

Roxanne laughed. "I wouldn't worry about that. A few extra pounds won't matter."

"Great! I wasn't looking forward to starving myself."

Wendy chuckled. Her daughter was as thin as a rake, even though she had a voracious appetite. "I don't think there's any chance of that. Come on, get dressed and I'll buy you lunch."

While Roxanne helped Natalie out of the gown, Wendy inspected the bridesmaids' dresses, which Roxanne also had designed. Paige, Wendy's youngest daughter, had been less than co-operative and showed little interest in her sister's wedding, turning up only once for a fitting. Wendy sometimes wondered if she'd even turn up for the wedding. She sighed heavily. It wasn't helpful comparing her children, but Natalie and Paige were so different. And then there was Simon...

"See you next time." Roxanne waved as Wendy and Natalie headed for the door.

"We'll look forward to it." Wendy smiled and then followed Natalie to the lift. While they waited, Wendy slipped her arm around Natalie's waist. "I'm sorry I get teary so often. It's... well, you know?"

"It's okay Mum. I understand. I wish Dad was here, too."

"I know you do, sweetheart."

The lift arrived and the doors opened. Stepping inside, they rode down the four levels, emerging into the foyer of the high-end building in downtown Sydney.

"Where would you like to go?" Wendy asked.

Natalie shrugged. "I don't mind, your choice."

"Okay. I know just the place." Wendy linked her arm through Natalie's and together they headed out into the bustling city. Taxis honked, moving like snails through the congested streets. Shoppers strolled along the footpath, chatting, pausing to look in shop windows, oblivious of the office workers weaving around them, hurrying to grab a quick midday meal before returning to their respective offices for the afternoon.

The aroma of freshly baked pizza wafted from an Italian restaurant, mingling with the scent of hot dogs piled high on a vendor's cart at the corner of Edward and King. "I wouldn't mind pizza," Natalie remarked, looking longingly over her shoulder while they waited for the lights to change.

"That's not really what I had in mind," Wendy said.

"What's wrong with pizza?"

Wendy laughed. "Nothing. Nothing at all. You know how much I love Italian food. I was just thinking of your waistline and your wedding dress." Wendy paused and then leaned in close to her daughter. "To be quite honest, I'm mostly worried about the mother-of-the-bride dress!"

The lights changed and Natalie giggled as they joined the crush of pedestrians crossing to the other side. They walked on in comfortable silence, Natalie seemingly content to follow Wendy, and several minutes later, they arrived at one of Wendy's favourite restaurants. One she and Greg had dined at often. Maybe it wasn't the wisest choice, but she couldn't think of a nicer place to lunch with her daughter.

When the maître d' greeted them, Wendy asked for an outdoor table.

"Of course, Mrs. Miller, follow me," the smartly dressed young woman replied.

Natalie raised a brow at her mother and walked beside her to the table on the balcony that the maître d' chose for them. After the young woman settled them in and promised to send a waiter to take their orders, Natalie leaned forward. "We didn't have to come here, Mum. It'll cost a fortune!"

"It's okay, darling. I wanted to spoil you," Wendy replied, trying hard to keep her voice steady. The restaurant had one of the best views of the harbour and the Opera House, and on this perfect spring day, the water glistening in the sunshine was just glorious. Just like the days when she and Greg came here…

"You don't need to," Natalie replied. She grew silent for a few seconds, her face paling. Grabbing Wendy's arm, she asked, "Are you okay, Mum?"

Wendy frowned. "Of course I am. What makes you think I'm not?"

"You look tired, that's all. And bringing me here…" Natalie's voice trailed away, but Wendy could see fear in her daughter's eyes.

"You wonder if I'm sick?"

"Yes."

Wendy squeezed Natalie's hand. "I'm fine. Nothing to worry about. Honestly."

"Are you sure?" Natalie asked, frowning.

"Positive!"

A male waiter approached and stopped beside the table. The two women grabbed their menus and quickly perused them.

"Are you ready to order, ladies, or shall I come back?" the well-groomed, dark-haired young man asked politely.

"Could you give us a few minutes, please?" Wendy removed her designer sunglasses and smiled at him.

"Of course." He poured two glasses of water from the jug on the table and stepped aside.

"There's no pizza on the menu," Natalie whispered loudly.

Wendy laughed. "You don't need pizza, Natalie."

"I know." Natalie chuckled. "Shall we share the paella instead?"

Wendy set her menu on the table and smiled lovingly at her daughter. "Good choice." She waved the waiter over and placed the order. After he left, she slipped her sunglasses back on, sipped her water, and studied her daughter. What would she do without Natalie? Soon, her eldest daughter would be married and have less time to spend with her mother. The thought saddened Wendy, but she knew she had to deal with it. She couldn't, but more importantly, wouldn't, impose on Natalie and Adam. The first year of marriage was such a special time. Even now, after all the years that had passed, memories of her first year with Greg filled her with such warmth. They'd had a wonderful marriage. But it was no good constantly reminiscing. Although he'd be waiting for her in the life to come, he was gone from this earth, and she had to accept that fact and try to build a new life on her own.

"Have you spoken to Simon lately?" Natalie asked.

Wendy blinked and returned her attention to Natalie. "Not for a few weeks. He's replied to a few texts, but I think he's super busy with work. Did you know he got a promotion?"

Natalie frowned again. "No. He's always busy when I call. Makes me think he doesn't want to talk to me anymore."

"You know your brother. When he doesn't want to talk, he doesn't want to talk. But when he chooses to, you can't stop him."

"Yes, but surely he can find time to talk to *you* at least once a week. You're his mother, after all."

"I've come to the conclusion that we have to give him space," Wendy replied as positively as she could, because, the truth was, she also wondered why Simon found it so hard to keep in touch, but she *was* his mother, and she wouldn't speak ill of him with his sister.

Natalie crossed her arms. "If he keeps this up much longer, I'm going to drive to his house and make him talk. I mean it!"

"Don't be like that, sweetheart. He doesn't like it when we pressure him, you know that."

"I don't understand him! You'd think with Dad gone, he'd be more attentive of you."

"I can look after myself. But I agree, it'd be lovely to see more of him."

The waiter approached and set the paella on the table between them. "Would you like me to serve?" he asked.

Wendy flashed an appreciative smile. "We'll be fine, thanks. It smells wonderful."

The waiter nodded, refilled their glasses, and wished them *bon appétit* before leaving them to their meal.

"Pass your plate, Mum," Natalie said, holding her hand out.

Wendy complied and Natalie heaped several spoons of the colourful dish onto the middle of the plate. Wendy held her hand up. "That's plenty, darling. Thank you."

"Are you sure? There's a lot here."

"Yes, that's fine."

Natalie filled her plate and then quickly scooped a huge spoonful into her mouth, releasing a pleasurable sigh. Wendy was glad the conversation about Simon had been dropped. His lack of communication did worry her, and she often wondered if something was wrong, but didn't want Natalie concerned about him with her wedding fast approaching. Wendy decided to call him again when she got home.

After making quick work of the paella, Natalie leaned back in her chair and placed her hands across her stomach. "So, what have you decided about the trip?"

Wendy sipped her iced tea and released a long sigh. Greg's grandmother, who lived just south of London, was turning ninety, and Wendy had booked a trip to the U.K. to attend the celebration. She'd also invited her friend, Robyn, to accompany her, but now Robyn couldn't go because her mother had taken ill, and Wendy was considering cancelling. She set her glass on the table and toyed with her fork. "I don't think I'll go."

"Oh Mum, I think you should. Since Dad's death, you've hardly taken a holiday—I think it'll do you good."

"But on my own?"

Natalie chuckled. "You never know, you might meet a handsome gentleman who'll sweep you off your feet!"

"Natalie!"

"Sorry…" A playful grin had spread across Natalie's face. She leaned forward, crossing her arms on the table. "Seriously, I think you should go. You've travelled a lot, you'll be fine. You need to go, Mum."

Wendy sighed heavily. "I'll give it some more thought. If I stay home, I can help more with the wedding preparations."

"You've already done more than enough. It's all in hand," Natalie replied with just a hint of exasperation in her voice.

"I know. But it seems strange to think of travelling to the other side of the world without your dad. It won't be the same."

Natalie squeezed her mother's hand. "I know. But go. Do it for Dad."

Wendy grimaced and swallowed the lump in her throat. "I'll think about it, but right now, I think I'd like coffee. Would you like one?"

"That would be lovely. Thank you."

Wendy beckoned the waiter over and ordered two cups.

"And can I tempt you with the dessert menu?" He quirked a brow as he held out two.

Wendy smiled politely. "Thank you, but no. Coffee will be fine."

Natalie leaned forward again after the waiter left, her face filled with disappointment. "I was going to order something," she said in a sulky tone.

Wendy chuckled, shaking her head. "You do take after your father with your sweet tooth."

"I can't help it," Natalie replied defensively, but then she laughed.

"I guess not. But even though Roxanne said it didn't matter, you should still watch what you're eating." Wendy quickly bit her lip. She shouldn't have said that. Natalie was a grown woman and could make her own decisions about what to eat and what to avoid. Thank goodness Natalie had an understanding nature. Paige would never have let her get away with saying anything like that. "I'm sorry darling. Have whatever you want." Wendy smiled and beckoned the waiter again.

CEDAR SPRINGS RANCH, TEXAS

Bruce McCarthy swung his legs off the bed and glanced at his watch. *Three p.m.* Releasing a slow breath, he ran his hand over his still thick, but graying hair. He really had to stop falling asleep in the afternoons—it was such a waste of time. However, now his eldest son, Nate, was running the ranch and insisted he take it easy, Bruce often found his eyes drooping in the early afternoon following their substantial mid-day meal, and he usually succumbed to a nap. However, he wasn't tired—he was just bored.

At sixty-three years of age, Bruce wasn't old, but his brush with bowel cancer a year earlier had shaken his sons, especially Nate. Although he'd beaten the disease, Nate had placed him on light duties, but Bruce was bored to tears. Retirement didn't suit him. He'd much rather be out tending cattle instead of looking after the books, which had never been one of his strong points.

A tentative knock sounded on the door. "Dad..." It was Nate, whispering in a low voice.

"Come in, son." Bruce pushed to his feet and crossed the room, grabbing a bottle of water from a small refrigerator tucked in a corner.

The door opened and Nate poked his rugged, good-looking cowboy head inside. "I'm heading to the bank in a few minutes. Need anything?"

Bruce shook his head. "I'm fine, thanks. I'm going to town soon, anyway."

Nate's forehead creased. "Sure you're up to it?"

Bruce did his best to hide his annoyance at his son's remark. He didn't need molly-coddling—the doctor had given him a clean bill of health. If only Nate wouldn't worry so much. And it was only a meeting at church to discuss fund-raising for the upgrade of the children's ministry hall. He wasn't about to do the actual renovations. "Of course I'm up to it," he replied with a reassuring smile before taking a slug of water. He didn't mention to Nate the other thing he was doing in town. He'd save that for later, when it was all sorted and too late to do anything about.

After Nate closed the door, Bruce sat at his desk and opened the drawer, taking out the itinerary the young woman at the travel agency had drawn up for him a few days earlier. He'd sworn her to secrecy. If Nate knew he was planning a trip to Ireland and England on his own, Bruce knew it was unlikely he'd even reach the airport lounge, let alone board the plane. But could he do it? He'd always thought that when he retired, he and his wife, Faith, would travel the world together, but Faith had passed on ten years earlier. Now, the choice was to go on his own or not at all.

Bruce re-read the itinerary. First stop, Ireland, the land of his forebears. His grandfather, Edward Bruce McCarthy, emigrated from Ireland in his early twenties, bought Cedar Springs Ranch and never returned. However, he never forgot his homeland and told endless tales and stories about the beautiful green isle. Ireland, Edward had told his young grandson, was a land filled with poets and fables, dreamers and agitators. Edward had sown a seed in the young Bruce's mind, and he wanted to see it for himself. He'd recently decided that now was the perfect time to visit the land he'd heard so much about, and maybe try to find some family members at the same time.

To Bruce it made perfect sense to go. He wasn't needed on the ranch, and after his health scare, every day was a blessing, and he wanted to make the most of the precious gift of life. Yes, he'd do it. He'd make the booking, pay for it, and then tell the family.

AFTER DROPPING Natalie outside her apartment block, Wendy continued on to her home at Cremorne, a suburb on the northern side of Sydney Harbour. It still was, and always had been, a lovely family home. She and Greg bought it soon after they married and had raised their children there. However, the memories could sometimes be overwhelming and the sprawling three-level home with views over the glistening harbour seemed so big and quiet now that only she and Paige lived there. But since Paige was rarely at home, it was almost as if Wendy lived alone, and that made the house seem even larger and emptier.

She turned her car into the driveway, waved to Rose, her elderly neighbour who looked up from her gardening and smiled, and then drove into the double garage. Stepping out of the car, the boxes stacked against one side of the garage wall caught Wendy's attention. Simon's... She let out a sigh. Would he ever collect them? She'd given him several ultimatums but hadn't the heart to follow through with tossing his things out when he hadn't come for them by the appointed date. She sighed again and unlocked the internal door leading to the house. It didn't matter. It wasn't as if the space was being used for anything else. Paige didn't have a car, and Wendy had finally sold Greg's large SUV just last year, so there really was no need to hassle Simon.

Pushing the door open, Wendy stepped into the house, set her bag on the kitchen counter, and filled the kettle. A faint meow sounded from the sunroom, and moments later, Muffin, Wendy's large, fluffy Persian, rubbed against her legs. Wendy bent down and picked him up, gave him a cuddle, and then set him back on the floor while she made a cup of tea.

After turning on some background music to cover the silence that always filled the rambling house these days, she carried her tea to the sunroom and sat in her favourite chair. Muffin immediately joined her and settled on her lap.

Opening the book she'd begun the night before, Wendy began reading while sipping her tea. She soon closed it when she found herself re-reading the same paragraph several times. Her focus was elsewhere. Having all but decided to cancel the trip to London, the conversation with Natalie now had her mind awhirl. Maybe she should go. Could Natalie be right, that it might do her good? Her gaze travelled to the large family photo on the far wall, taken not long before Greg passed away unexpectedly. They all looked so happy, and they *had* been. Such a different story now. Paige hadn't coped well with her father's sudden death and blamed God for letting him die before his time. Simon had withdrawn further. Natalie did what she always did and soldiered on. They all had their own ways of coping. Wendy drew comfort and strength from quiet times spent in the Word, her family, her church, and her work as a part-time University Lecturer. But she still missed Greg terribly. She guessed she always would.

She reached for the travel pack the agent had given her and flicked through the itinerary. She and Robyn had planned to visit Ireland before flying to England. Greg had always wanted to visit the emerald isle. Wendy wasn't sure what had sparked his interest, but he'd always promised they'd go, and she'd been looking forward to seeing it. But could she do it on her own? Would it make her miss him more, or would it help her let go and move on? She drew a deep breath and closed her eyes, fingering the cross around her neck. *Lord, I'm really struggling with this—please show me what to do. You know how much I miss Greg, and how heavy my heart is when I think about travelling to the other side of the world without him, but maybe I should go. Please help me draw strength from You, and please guide and direct me. In Jesus' precious name. Amen.*

Half an hour later, after finishing her tea and finally finishing a chapter of her book, inexplicable peace flooded Wendy's heart. She made up her mind. She'd go to the birthday party in London, and to Ireland. She'd do it for Greg, but also for herself. She needed to start making a life for herself without him, because deep down, she knew that the loneliness that was her constant companion wouldn't leave until she did. Clinging to memories, as wonderful as they were, wouldn't help her move forward. Taking this trip, no matter how challenging it might be, would be a start to building a new life. Drawing a resolved breath, she picked up the phone and called the travel agent.

CHAPTER 2

*H*aving made the decision to go, Wendy wasted no time in finalising her travel plans. Although Robyn was unable to go with her, Wendy was truly grateful and relieved when her friend kindly offered to look after Muffin as Wendy couldn't trust Paige to look after her precious cat.

It grieved her greatly that her youngest daughter had gone off the rails since Greg's passing, staying out until all hours, night after night, and sometimes not making it home at all. It wasn't how she and Greg had raised their children. Wendy constantly prayed that Paige would return to her faith and change her ways, and she trusted God would keep working on her. In the meantime, she often struggled to control her tongue and not say things that would upset her feisty daughter and alienate her further. Paige was one of the reasons she finally decided to take the trip. Something told her that her daughter needed to know what it truly felt like to be responsible for herself and not have her mother pick up the pieces from the messes she made. How many times had Paige shouted at her that she 'just wanted to be left alone', or, 'why didn't she just let her live her own life'? Wendy had no intention of doing either, but maybe a few weeks of being on her own might help Paige come to her senses and see her family's love and support in a different light. Wendy could only hope and pray.

The day before Wendy was due to fly out, Natalie organised a farewell dinner at her apartment. Wendy was surprised, but pleased, that both Simon and Paige had come. She'd had a few brief conversations with her son over the past week or so, but he always seemed too busy to meet or to have a longer chat. But he was here tonight, and he and Adam, Natalie's fiancé, were deep in conversation on the balcony. She would have loved to have a more in-depth talk with her son, but she was pleased that he was at least chatting with someone. It was a good thing that Adam was a sensible, stable, Christian man. He and Natalie were so well suited, and Wendy knew they'd have a happy marriage. Adam could be a very good influence on her son, but she wouldn't push it. She was learning that sometimes it was best to let things happen and not force them. Pray about them, and then leave them with God.

Natalie gave her a big hug and offered to take her bag. "Can I get you a drink, Mum?"

"A cup of tea would be lovely, dear. I've had such a busy day."

Natalie laughed. "I'm sure you have. There's always so much to do before a trip."

"Yes, it would have been better if I was going during the

mid-term break," Wendy said with a sigh as she handed her bag to Natalie.

"Oh Mum, everyone will cope without you. Don't worry."

Natalie was right. At work, she'd be easily replaced, but she wasn't so sure how Paige would survive without her. She made a mental note to ask Natalie to keep an eye on her younger sister, but Wendy also needed to trust God to look after Paige and to work in her life. And try not to worry. Wendy stepped towards Paige and slipped her arm around her waist and popped a kiss on her translucent cheek. "Good to see you, darling."

Natalie frowned. "You two live in the same house, don't you?"

"Yes, but we're like ships in the night, aren't we?" Wendy said, swallowing a lump in her throat as she smiled at Paige.

Paige ignored her mother's smile and simply shrugged off-handedly. "We see each other enough."

Paige's petulant tone and expression saddened Wendy. She drew a steadying breath and determined not to make a fuss on the night before she was to leave. She was also glad that Natalie didn't make any further comment.

Placing the tea on the kitchen counter, Natalie nodded towards the balcony. "Simon came."

"Yes, I saw him when I came in. You did well."

Natalie winced. "It wasn't easy. I don't know what his problem is."

"Why don't you both just leave him alone?" Paige hissed before shrugging Wendy's arm off and making her way towards the kitchen. She headed straight to the fridge, her face

17

quickly taking on a look of disgust when she opened it. "Where's the beer, sis?"

"We don't drink, Paige. You know that." Natalie's voice was controlled but firm.

"But I do." Paige pursed her lips and slammed the fridge door.

Wendy caught Natalie's gaze and gave her head a discreet shake.

Natalie's eyes narrowed and her jaw tightened. Paige's behaviour also grieved her, and Wendy knew she would want to reprimand her sister, so relief filled her when Natalie responded calmly, "I'm sorry, Paige. I should have thought. We've got ginger beer."

Paige shuddered. "I'll go get a six-pack."

Wendy went to grab Paige's arm, but at the last moment, refrained. They'd had too many run-ins over Paige's alcohol intake—making a scene here would achieve nothing. Instead, she asked her not to be long, but Wendy knew that once outside the apartment, Paige might not return. It was a risk.

"I won't. The shop's only at the corner." Paige pursed her lips and made a bee-line for the door.

"Okay. See you soon," Wendy called after her, silently praying that her daughter would decide to return and not disappear into the night.

She picked up her tea, sipped it, and stepped closer to Natalie. "Can you and Adam keep an eye on her while I'm gone?"

"Of course, Mum. She's a worry, isn't she?"

"She is. She's still angry with God, but it's been four years now."

"I think she's angry with everyone," Natalie replied with sadness in her voice.

"You might be right. We'll have to pray harder."

"Yes, we will. But don't worry. Adam and I will keep an eye out." Natalie grabbed the oven mitts and opened the oven, pulling out a freshly cooked, home-made pizza before slipping another in. "Hope you don't mind—we're having pizza." She flashed a playful grin.

Wendy shook her head and chuckled. "They smell wonderful."

Natalie smiled. "I hope they taste as good."

"I'm sure they will." Wendy gave Natalie's shoulder a squeeze and smiled when Adam and Simon wandered in from outside. Setting her tea down, she extended her arms to them both. "Ah, my two favourite men in the entire world!" She gave Simon a hug and a kiss and then turned to Adam.

Her future son-in-law bent down and kissed her cheek. "Good to see you, Wendy. All packed and ready to go?"

"I think so, but I'll check again tonight."

"And you'll probably do it again in the morning," Simon said, giving her a knowing look.

Wendy chuckled. Despite not seeing much of each other in recent times, her son knew her very well. "Yes, no doubt I will. So, how's your job going?" She desperately hoped he'd chat with her and not shut her out. Her heart ached for him. Although he appeared normal, she knew something was going on. She was his mother, after all.

"Busy."

"I know that," she said softly.

He shrugged. "Not much else to tell, really."

Wendy tried to hide her disappointment. Why wouldn't he talk? "You're enjoying it?"

"Yes." He picked up a handful of nuts, threw his head back, and tossed them into his mouth casually, but Wendy sensed he was on full alert and the casualness was just an act. Something was worrying him. If only she knew what it was.

"Adam, can you help me?" Natalie called from the kitchen, waving a pizza cutter.

"Sure." Adam stepped away, leaving Wendy alone with Simon. She was positive he was hiding something and was itching to quiz him, but instinctively knew it was the wrong thing to do. She was even hesitant to ask if he still had the girlfriend he'd brought to Christmas, but then asked anyway.

"No. We broke up a while ago," he replied matter-of-factly.

"You're not seeing anyone, then?" Wendy asked the question but knew his answer before he even replied.

"Not at the moment." His jaw tightened. Wendy had no idea why he'd have trouble keeping a girlfriend. He took after his father with smooth, olive skin and classically handsome features; he was well-educated, smart, and hard-working, or had been until he quit university two years earlier and took a mundane job in a convenience store. She still had no understanding as to why he'd done that. However, since being at the store, he'd worked through the ranks and was now the area manager, which showed his determination to succeed. Of course, it was nothing compared to the career he *could* have had, and still could have, if he wanted it.

It grieved her that she didn't know how to reach him, and that she really didn't know him anymore. Over the last few years it felt like she was holding a polite conversation with a stranger, not her son. Maybe his tight-lipped behaviour was the reason he had little success in the dating department. But then, maybe he just hadn't met the right girl. After all, she and Greg hadn't married until they were in their late twenties. They'd both been career people, but when they met at a conference on the Gold Coast, she'd known from that moment that she'd happily put her career as a History teacher on hold to be his wife. Simon wasn't twenty-five, so he still had plenty of time.

"I'm sure you'll find someone soon," she said as she rubbed his arm.

He gave her an off-handed smile, as if to humour her.

She grimaced. She really needed to step back and not attempt to control the lives of her children. Not that she meant to, but it was hard to let go, to allow them to make their own choices and decisions, and mistakes. She wanted them to be happy, but she knew, *she really knew*, that they had to find their own way. However, if ever they needed her, she'd be there at the drop of a hat.

The door opened and Paige re-entered, six-pack in hand. Everyone turned and stared at her.

"Have I got two heads or something?" she snarled.

Wendy sighed. "No need for that, darling."

"Well, stop looking at me." Paige flicked everyone an annoyed look.

"Well, my dear sister, if you hadn't dyed your hair bright pink, we might look elsewhere." Simon laughed with amusement and quirked a brow.

"If you'd keep your mouth shut, that would be good!" Paige snapped.

21

"Paige. That's enough! Stop acting like a spoiled brat." Natalie glared at her.

Adam, always the peace-maker, stepped forward, holding his arms out. "Come on, everyone. Let's stop this nonsense. Don't spoil Wendy's last night before she leaves."

"Yeah, and who makes you the good cop?" Paige put the six-pack down and took a beer. "Anyone else want one?"

"I will." Simon held his hand out.

"Are you going to be nice to me?" Paige narrowed her eyes.

"Sure."

She handed him one. "Anyone else?"

Paige was baiting them. She was good at it. Wendy wouldn't bite, and she hoped Natalie wouldn't, either. She was relieved when Adam thanked her but said they'd stick with the soft stuff.

"Suit yourself." Paige opened the fridge and put the remaining four bottles inside.

"Dinner's ready," Natalie announced in a high-pitched voice. Having a family meal shouldn't have been stressful, and if Greg had been there, it would have been a wonderful, fun-filled evening. But he wasn't. Somehow, the family had to pull together without him, but Wendy knew it might take some-thing special to make that happen. It pained her that Greg's death hadn't drawn them closer. Instead, since his passing, a chasm had grown between them and it seemed to be deepening.

"Everyone, take a seat. Adam will give thanks," Natalie continued.

Wendy caught Adam's gaze and smiled. She was so thankful

he'd taken on the role as head of the family although he was yet to officially join it.

They all sat and bowed their heads. In years gone by, they would have held hands, but those years had long gone and it saddened Wendy deeply.

Adam cleared his throat. "Lord God, we give You thanks for all the good things You bless us with. Thank You for family, and for Wendy's trip. Keep her safe and let her have a wonderful time. And thank You for this food. In Jesus' name. Amen."

Wendy smiled when both Paige and Simon said 'Amen', although she knew it was out of habit. Their family had always given thanks at meal time, but it was good to see they hadn't forgotten. There was hope for them both, she knew that, and she would never give up praying for them.

The pizza tasted as good at it smelled. Paige and Simon behaved after having another beer each, and Natalie and Adam were attentive hosts. Despite their differences and troubles, Wendy would miss them all, but she knew deep down it was time to venture out on her own and to leave her children to fend for themselves for a while.

They said their farewells that evening. Simon, Natalie and Adam were unable to see her off at the airport due to work commitments. Paige had agreed to drive her since she had no lectures at Uni until the afternoon. Wendy almost changed her mind about going when Natalie hugged her and wished her a happy and safe trip. Until then, it hadn't been real. Was she really doing the right thing, leaving her family and travelling half-way around the world without Greg by her side? How would she manage all the transfers and check-ins without him?

"We'll be fine, Mum. Go and enjoy yourself."

Wendy sighed and pulled her daughter close. "I'll be praying for you."

Natalie pulled back and held her mother at arms' length. "Thank you. Now, off you go. I'm sure you'll have a wonderful time."

Wendy smiled. "I hope so." She then turned to Simon and held her hands out, pushing tears back. "It was lovely to see you tonight." Her voice faltered and tears stung her eyes.

He stepped forward and wrapped his arms around her. "Have a good time, Mum. I love you."

Wendy's heart almost crumbled. "I love you, too, Simon. Look after yourself, okay?"

"I will," he answered. She saw Greg in his smile and it ripped at her heart.

CHAPTER 3

The following morning, Wendy rose before dawn, showered, dressed in the comfortable travel clothes she'd set out the night before, and rechecked her bag twice. Ready an hour early, she made another coffee and checked her itinerary and tickets again while waiting for Paige to get ready.

Once in the car, Paige barely said a word. Wendy tried to make conversation, but Paige was either concentrating on her driving, understandable given she was in her mother's car in rush hour traffic, or she was in a bad mood. Wendy assumed it was a bit of both and didn't push her.

Arriving at the airport, Paige parked Wendy's car in the multi-level car park, and then helped with the bags before they headed to the departure hall. The place buzzed with people like Wendy, about to leave Australian shores for countries far afield and family members, like Paige, seeing them off before returning to their everyday lives.

After Wendy checked in, she suggested they grab a coffee

since she still had plenty of time. Paige agreed. They placed their order and sat at a table overlooking the runway. Wendy sipped her coffee and glanced at her daughter.

Paige's eyes narrowed. "What are you looking at?"

"Just wondering what colour your hair will be when I get back. That's all," Wendy replied gently.

"Dwayne likes it pink." Paige held Wendy's gaze, baiting her.

"Right..." Dwayne was Paige's latest boyfriend. Not one of Wendy's favourites, but Paige seemed to go out of her way to choose boyfriends her family wouldn't approve of. Not that Wendy ever voiced her disapproval—she knew better than that, but Paige's choices concerned her. Wendy prayed she'd find another Adam, but then, Paige wasn't Natalie. Wendy inhaled slowly. She had to trust God to work in her daughter's heart, to bring her back to Himself, and trust that in the meantime, she'd make good choices. She smiled. "Pink suits you."

"Thanks." Paige sipped her coffee and twiddled a strand of hair.

"I'm going to miss you," Wendy said softly.

Their gazes connected, and for a fleeting moment, Wendy saw the little girl Paige used to be and her throat thickened. A beautiful, dark-haired child, Paige loved cuddles and couldn't wait to be read to at bedtime. Out of the three children, she was the one who always offered to pray first.

Wendy now prayed silently for her precious baby girl as she struggled to contain her emotion. *Lord, care for Paige in my absence. Let her know that You love her more than anything, and that even though we don't understand why, that You had a purpose in allowing Greg to die. Please let her see You as a loving Heavenly Father who only wants the best for her. Thank You, dear Lord.*

Paige turned her head and stared out the window, lifting her chin stubbornly. She was protecting her heart, but there was no need. If only she knew how much she was loved.

Wendy squeezed Paige's forearm gently and finished her coffee. "It's time for me to go. Thanks for driving me, sweetheart."

Paige sniffed and turned her head. "You're welcome."

They stood. Wendy pulled her daughter close and hugged her. "I love you, Paige."

"I love you, too, Mum." The words were soft, barely audible, but she said them, filling Wendy with hope and warming her heart.

Wendy reluctantly drew back, smiled, and took a steadying breath before turning and striding to the boarding gate before she changed her mind.

THE LONG-HAUL FLIGHT was made bearable by the attentive hostesses and her Premium Economy seat, affordable, thanks to Greg's insurance money. However, Wendy would have much preferred to be uncomfortable in Economy and have him beside her.

She chatted with the youth in the seat to her left on and off throughout the journey. Johnno told her he was starting a twelve-month working holiday and he eagerly quizzed her on all the places she'd travelled to. As she shared with him, memories of the year she and Greg worked and lived in London soon after they were married flooded back, filling her with nostalgia. Greg had worked for a high-end Accountancy firm and was offered a transfer to the London branch for a year, which they accepted. Having family to live with enabled them to save enough money to set themselves up for life. It wasn't the same experience her flying companion would have. She'd heard stories of young Aussies living on vegemite sandwiches for weeks on end because they were paid so poorly. She could imagine Paige being one of them should she choose to take a gap year.

It was nice having someone to chat with, but Johnno wasn't Greg, so instead of resting her head on her husband's shoulder to sleep as she'd done in the past, Wendy did her best to stay upright in her own seat and tried to squelch the feelings of loneliness that knocked on her subconscious and once again made her question the wisdom of embarking on this trip alone.

More than a whole day and night later, she arrived in Dublin. Although she and Greg were seasoned travellers, she'd booked a transfer to her hotel. She could afford it, and the thought of finding her own way in a strange city after such a long flight didn't appeal.

The 'Hotel Shelton' was exactly how she expected an Irish hotel to be. Framed pictures of leprechauns and shamrocks adorned the walls, the carpet was green and the aroma of Guinness wafted from the bar.

As soon as she checked in and entered her room, fresh waves of nostalgia threatened to overwhelm. Her first hotel room without Greg. She'd almost become used to living on her own, but experiencing new places without him was entirely different, especially when he'd always dreamed of visiting

Ireland. They should have done it when they lived so close in London, all those years ago. Wendy didn't know why they hadn't. She guessed they thought they had all the time in the world.

Removing her scarf, her gaze travelled around the room. Tastefully furnished, it appeared comfortable and homey. The chintz curtains, plump cushions and four-poster bed suited the period building.

After the porter set her luggage on the stand and left the room, she inhaled deeply and began unpacking. She could do this. It wasn't how she'd planned to see Ireland, but she'd do it for Greg—and for herself. He'd want her to enjoy her time away, and so, as she stepped into the shower to freshen up, she determined to do just that. No more melancholy. No more nostalgia. She would live in the present, not the past. She'd be thankful for all her blessings, past, present and future. God still had a purpose and a plan for her life. She'd face the future with anticipation, and trust God to lead her to new things.

As the warm water refreshed her body, songs of worship refreshed her soul, and when she stepped out of the shower, she was ready to embrace whatever God had in mind for her.

Dressing in comfortable trousers and a long-sleeved shirt, Wendy grabbed a jacket before heading out to explore the sights of Dublin. Tomorrow she'd do it properly, catch one of those hop-on, hop-off tourist buses, but for now, she'd stroll around the surrounding streets and get a feel for the city before an early dinner and bed.

She grabbed a handy map from the hotel reception desk before stepping out onto busy O'Connell Street. She headed towards the River Liffey, but the side streets, with their bohemian, friendly atmosphere, soon beckoned and she quickly became lost in the maze of narrow streets, laughing when she came face to face with the statue of Molly Malone and her famous wheelbarrow. Greg would have loved it.

Reaching the river, she strolled across the pedestrian only Ha'penny Bridge. Built in 1816, it was originally a toll bridge that cost half a penny to cross—hence its name. Wendy stopped in the middle and took photos of the river and the city before continuing on. With evening fast approaching, the Temple Bar area on the other side of the river already teemed with tourists, street entertainers, Irish music, and greeters dressed as leprechauns standing outside the multitude of restaurants and pubs, thrusting menus in peoples' faces to entice them inside to eat. Wendy smiled and said "No, thanks" politely so many times that she finally gave up and simply ignored them. They were only doing their jobs, but she'd rather not be harassed.

Weariness overtook her, and she decided the simplest option was to eat in the hotel's dining room. After the noise and bustle of the tourist area, it was a relief to sit at a quiet table with a cup of tea while she waited for her meal to arrive. She took the opportunity to post some photos on her Face-book profile and send messages to the children. Not that they were children, but she still thought of them as such. Her message to each simply read: *Survived my first day... Dublin's an interesting city, but I'm looking forward to bed before exploring it more tomorrow. Hope all is well. Love you, Mum xx*

Natalie and Simon replied almost immediately; Paige's lack of reply didn't overly concern her, it was normal, but Wendy did wonder what her youngest daughter was doing that she couldn't reply. She tried not to worry.

The following morning, after a wonderful sleep, Wendy dressed for the day and headed downstairs to the hotel's restaurant for breakfast. After settling down with a bowl of cereal, some fruit, and a cup of coffee, she was engrossed in her daily devotional when her elbow was bumped. Warm liquid splashed her hand, hit her leg, and seeped through her skirt onto her thigh. Startled, she looked up.

A man in a cowboy hat had stopped and began to apologize profusely. Quickly grabbing a handful of napkins from the dispenser, he pressed some into her hand and mopped the pool of coffee on the table with the rest. "I'm sorry. I'm not sure how that happened." His gentlemanly southern twang intrigued her and brought a smile to her lips.

She dabbed her thigh. "It's okay. At least it wasn't hot."

"I'm not usually so clumsy. Let me get you another coffee."

She smiled again, taking note of his sparkling blue eyes. "There's really no need."

"But I'd like to." His smile was as charming as his voice, and when their gazes met, her heart jolted, taking her by surprise.

She swallowed hard and replied, "If you insist. Thank you."

"Sure. I'll be right back."

As he walked away, Wendy wiped the cover of her book and couldn't keep the grin off her face. Something about him made her heart beat a little faster. The twinkle in his eyes? The softness of his voice? She laughed at herself. What would Greg think? One handsome stranger spilling coffee on her and she was acting like a giddy teenager instead of the grown middle-aged woman that she was. She got a grip on herself and returned to her devotion, although she couldn't stop herself from glancing up every few words to see if he was returning with her fresh coffee.

When he returned and set the cup on the table, she smiled and thanked him, glanced quickly at his left hand to make sure he wasn't wearing a wedding band, and then surprised herself by asking if he'd like to join her.

"I wouldn't want to intrude."

She closed her book and set it aside. "You're not intruding."

"Well, that's very kind of you." He sat opposite, and looking up and meeting her gaze, extended his deep brown and slightly calloused hand. "I'm Bruce, by the way."

She smiled. "And I'm Wendy. It's nice to meet you." She tried to sound calm, but her voice betrayed her.

They chatted while sipping their coffees. He spoke calmly, but she could barely get two words out without her voice hitching.

He told her he was in Dublin trying to find relatives, and that he planned to visit England on his return trip to the States. She told him that she too was exploring Ireland before visiting England. "My late husband's grandmother is turning ninety, and I'm going to the party."

"That's a mighty milestone to be proud of."

"It sure is." Wendy sipped her coffee as memories of Greg's grandmother flitted across her mind. Greg's parents had moved to Australia before he was born, leaving both sets of parents behind in England, but during their year in London, when Greg and Wendy lived with his maternal grandmother, a bond had grown between them. Now that Greg's parents were also gone, Wendy felt truly honoured to share this special occasion with the elderly lady.

Bruce finished his coffee and stood, tipping his hat. "Have a good day, Wendy. And once again, I'm sorry."

"Oh, please don't worry about it. No harm done." She waved it off as if it was nothing. And it was. It really was. It had been a long time since she'd talked with a man she got on so well with. A tinge of regret squeezed her heart when she realised she'd probably not see him again.

"You're too kind." He smiled, hesitated, then cleared his throat. "I...I guess you wouldn't want to have supper with me tonight? It'd sure be nice to have your company."

Wendy blinked. Had she heard correctly? Had he just invited her to dinner? She blinked again. No, she hadn't misheard. Her heart pounded and her lips curved into a soft smile. "I'd love to. Thank you."

"Wonderful. I'll book for six-thirty. Shall we meet in the foyer at six?"

"Sounds perfect, I'll be there."

"I'll look forward to it," he said.

They exchanged phone numbers before he gave another smile, tipped his hat again, and then walked away.

Wendy remained in her seat, shocked, but slightly amused, by the turn of events. Was this a result of her letting go of the past and embracing the present? Whatever it was, her day had just become a lot brighter. She quickly saved his number to her list of contacts.

CHAPTER 4

*B*ruce had already spent several days, with little success, trying to locate his family, although he'd learned that the family had moved across town about thirty years earlier. Unfortunately, McCarthy was a common name, and he hadn't done enough research before he left home, assuming it would be easy to locate them. How wrong could he be? But still, he decided to try one last time.

Pulling out his phone, he searched for all the McCarthys in and near the suburb of Hollybrock, a southern suburb close to the sea. Ending up with a list of more than a hundred, he had a sinking feeling that finding a relative amongst them would be like finding a needle in a haystack. However, he began making the calls.

After twenty dead ends, he almost gave up. After thirty, he ordered another coffee. After forty, his thoughts turned to the woman he'd met that morning. He smiled to himself while anticipating having supper with her tonight.

He drained his coffee and called number forty-one. Yet again, the call resulted in another dead end, but the elderly man was up for a chat—not that Bruce could understand him.

As he mindlessly made the next batch of calls, his thoughts returned to Wendy. He'd been surprised, but pleased, that she'd accepted his invitation. Lost in thought, he almost missed hearing the voice on the other end of the phone. "Yes, I might be related to the McCarthys who used to live in Larch Hill."

Bruce blinked and quickly checked the list. Whom had he just called? "I'm sorry. What did you say your name was?"

"Aileen McCarthy." The elderly woman's accent was as broad as they came and he could barely understand her.

"My grandfather was Edward Bruce McCarthy," Bruce told her. "He left Ireland in his early twenties and emigrated to Texas."

"Edward Bruce," she mused. "I think he might be my father's brother, my uncle."

"Really?" Bruce thought quickly. "So, that makes you my…"

"First cousin, once removed."

"Yes…" This woman might be elderly, but there was nothing wrong with her mind—she was as sharp as a tack.

"We always wondered what happened to Uncle Edward," she said.

"Do you know why he left?" he asked.

"It's a long story."

He chuckled. "I've got all day."

"Come for a visit. I'll tell you all about it." Her voice hinted that something sinister may have happened. His grandfather hadn't mentioned anything bad that drove him away from his home, but then again, he'd never said much about his family at all. It had been like pulling teeth to learn anything about his family, even though he loved Ireland.

"I'd like that, but are you sure? You don't know me."

"I've been praying for this day for a long time."

Bruce's eyes shot open. "Okay." He confirmed her address and said he'd be there as soon as possible. Gathering his belongings, he dashed to his room and grabbed his coat, then quickly made his way down to the entrance and hailed a cab. He could have caught a bus, but this was too important an event to risk getting lost.

Half an hour later, the cab stopped in front of a neat, semi-detached home in a quiet, suburban street. He couldn't get over how narrow the street was. There was barely space for two cars to pass, nor could he get over how close the houses were. Where he came from, you couldn't even see your neighbor's house.

Bruce paid the driver and climbed out. During the ride he'd tried to imagine what his first cousin, once removed, would look like, but there was no need to imagine any longer—Aileen McCarthy was in the front garden tending to an array of colorful plants. Dressed in a long, brown skirt and a thick, plaid shawl that covered her shoulders, her silvery-gray hair was swept into a bun. Wispy strands of hair hung down her neck and cheeks. According to his calculations, she must have been close to one hundred, but she didn't appear that old. Straightening, her creased face lit up as he approached. "Come in, my dear boy."

He'd come home. After all this time of not knowing anything about his Irish family, suddenly, he'd found them, and he immediately felt he belonged. What a kindly old woman she was—his first cousin, once removed.

"Thank you." He stepped toward her and extended his hand. "It's lovely to meet you. I'm Bruce."

"I figured that." She chuckled as she shook his hand. "And I'm Aileen."

He chuckled too. "I figured that as well."

He offered to help her up the steps, but she said she could manage, and she did. If he could be as sprightly as her if he reached her age, he thought, he'd be happy.

She led him through the small porch and into a long, narrow hallway. A set of stairs came off to the side, but she walked past them and continued along the hallway which was covered in an almost threadbare red carpet until she reached a small sitting room beside the kitchen. "Take a seat while I make a pot of tea." Aileen gestured toward the table laden with homemade cookies and what looked like an Irish tea cake.

"Can I help?"

"That's kind of you, but I can manage." Obviously, Aileen was fiercely independent, just like his grandfather, and his father, and for that matter, himself and Nate. A family trait, it seemed.

While he sat and waited, Bruce gazed about the room. Dainty tea cups and ornaments filled a dresser on one wall. Ancient black and white photographs hung on the walls and perched on top of an old timber dresser. A framed picture of Mary and Jesus hung on another wall, and a well-worn Bible sat open on a side table. He gathered she lived alone, and given that none of the photos seemed to have been taken in recent years, he guessed she might not have had any children or grandchildren.

She carried the pot of tea to the table and joined him. "Let me pour," he said, holding the old woman's gaze and daring her to argue.

"If you insist." She chuckled, her wrinkled face breaking into a smile.

"I do." He proceeded to pour the tea into the dainty cups, setting one in front of her.

She lifted the cup to her lips and blew on the steaming beverage, taking a small sip before placing it back down. "So, you want to know about your grandfather?"

"I do."

A faraway look filled her face and Bruce settled in to hear the story of his family.

AFTER WENDY FINISHED her replacement coffee, she quickly headed back to her room to grab her jacket before walking outside to wait for the hop-on, hop-off bus. As she stood with several others, her phone rang. Scrambling in her bag, she pulled it out and frowned. Paige. After a quick calculation, she worked out it was midnight in Sydney. "Paige, hello…is everything okay?"

"Yes. I just miss you." She hiccupped into the phone.

Wendy winced. It was nice that Paige missed her, but it was disappointing to realise she was intoxicated. "I miss you too, darling. Where are you?"

"I've just got home." Hiccup. "Are you enjoying yourself?"

"I'm having a lovely time, thank you. Are you sure you're all right?"

"No..." Sobs replaced hiccups.

Wendy's heart constricted. What was she supposed to do from half-way around the world? "What's happened, darling?"

"Dwayne dumped me."

Wendy sighed with relief, thinking something worse might have happened, but obviously, it had upset Paige. "Oh sweetie, I'm so sorry."

"It's okay. I'll find someone else." Paige sniffed, hiccupped again.

Wendy sighed inwardly. If only Paige wouldn't jump into another relationship before she had time to get over this one, but it was what she did. It was her way of coping with her father's death, apparently.

After chatting a while longer, the bus arrived and Wendy promised Paige that she'd call back later. Taking a seat on the top deck, her heart was as heavy as the grey clouds that filled the Dublin skyline, and she prayed silently for her daughter as the bus slowly filled with tourists. There was nothing else she could do from half-way around the world, and besides, God was able to do far more than she could, but Wendy's heart ached for Paige, a hurting soul who blamed God for not healing her dad. Paige had been seventeen when Greg died, and she'd handled his death badly ever since. Much worse than Natalie and Simon. Not that they didn't grieve, but Paige's way of dealing with the loss of her dad was to party, drink and constantly have a boyfriend by her side.

Oh God, be with my baby. Let her know Your love and peace, and may she return to You and learn to love You. Heal her grieving heart, dear Lord. In Jesus' precious name. Amen.

During the tour, Paige was constantly on Wendy's mind. She didn't have a favourite child, but Paige had certainly captured her heart from the moment she came into the world. Her bubbly personality brightened everyone's day, her cute antics made Wendy and Greg laugh, and they thanked God every day for bringing her into their lives. Now, Wendy prayed every day that God would bring Paige back into the fold before she truly messed up her life. It saddened her that Paige blamed God for Greg's death. Paige had told Wendy in a drunken rage that 'she didn't want to love a God who promised life but then took it away'. Nothing Wendy had said to date had made her change her mind, so all she could do was pray that God would keep knocking on the door of her heart, and that one day, Paige would answer.

The day passed, and despite Paige never being far from Wendy's thoughts, she enjoyed the sights of Dublin. Her last stop was St. Stephens Green, and she was looking forward to strolling through the gardens she'd heard wonderful things about. After her walk through the gardens, she'd return to the hotel and take a short rest before dressing for dinner.

As she admired the Victorian layout of the green, with its perimeter trees and shrubs, the herbaceous borders bursting with colour, the waterfall and ornamental lake, as well as the sculptures scattered throughout the green, she also wondered at the wisdom of having dinner with a man she barely knew, and after tonight, would most likely never see again. Just as she was getting her phone out of her bag to phone Bruce and make an excuse to call off the date, it pinged. It was him, confirming the arrangements. It was too late... she'd have to go; it would be bad manners not to.

CHAPTER 5

*R*eturning to the hotel much later than expected, Bruce had just enough time to freshen up for his evening with Wendy. Aileen certainly knew how to talk, and what stories she'd told him. His mind was still reeling. He quickly showered and dressed in the smartest clothes he'd brought with him—black trousers, a crisp, white, button-up shirt, and a tan leather jacket. He would have been more comfortable in jeans and boots, but Wendy had been stylishly dressed when they met, so he wanted to look equally polished. He then hurried to the hotel foyer where they'd arranged to meet.

Stepping out of the elevator, he smiled. She was already there, looking like a million dollars in a cream cashmere sweater and a dark skirt that looked both sophisticated and warm and really suited her curvy figure.

When their gazes met, she waved and her face lit up. He approached her, smiling. "You look lovely. Sorry I'm late."

She returned his smile. "No need to apologize. Did you have a successful day?"

"Yes, I did. I'll tell you about it over supper."

She angled her head. "Can I ask a question?"

"Sure, ask away."

"Where are you from?"

He frowned. "Can't you tell?"

"Texas?" she asked tentatively.

"Yes, ma'am. You got it in one. And you're from down under, I reckon."

"My accent is a dead giveaway, right?" She let out a small chuckle.

Bruce shrugged and they both laughed. He was enjoying their easy banter. He offered his arm. "Shall we walk?"

"That would be lovely." She linked her arm through his and strolled beside him out of the hotel and onto the bustling street. It was early evening, and they weren't the only ones out for a stroll—it seemed that all of Dublin was out and about. Albeit, they were in the busy part of town, so it wasn't surprising. He pulled her out of the way of a youth on a skateboard, and they slowed when a couple in front stopped to look in a shop window. After several minutes, they reached a restaurant called "O'Leary's Bar and Brasserie", recommended to Bruce by the hotel concierge. Typically Irish from the outside, a plaque of a leprechaun swigging a Guinness swung from the roof, and baskets of brightly colored flowers hung from hooks along the wall and dotted the sidewalk.

Upon entering, he almost turned around and left. A number of young men sat at the bar. The first word he heard

43

was one he wouldn't want his grandchildren to hear, or Wendy, for that matter. He glanced at her, but she shrugged. They ventured further inside, his eyes slowly adapting to the darkened interior.

Reaching the restaurant area, Bruce spoke to the hostess and they followed the polite young woman to a table toward the rear where it was quieter and they could better appreciate the pianist who was playing the soft background music.

Within moments, a waitress approached and asked if she could get them anything to start with.

Bruce raised a brow at Wendy. "Would you like a drink?"

"I'd love a cup of tea."

"And I'll have the same, thank you." It seemed that Wendy didn't drink alcohol. He was pleased about that. Not that it bothered him when others partook, but he'd given it up several years earlier when he'd started drinking too much to help deal with his grief over losing Faith. After his cancer scare, he'd made an even bigger effort to eat and drink more healthily. A cup of tea would do him just fine.

"I'll be right back with your tea and to take your orders," the waitress said.

"Thank you kindly." With the waitress gone, Bruce turned his attention to Wendy. "How was your day?"

"Lovely, thank you. Dublin's an interesting city. However, you need to tell me what happened with you. Did you find your family?"

"I did. A cousin, first removed." He paused a moment and toyed with his fork before continuing. "So, it turns out my grandfather left Ireland because of a broken heart."

"Oh." Wendy sighed. "That's sad. And he never returned?"

"Never. From what my cousin, Aileen, understood, my grandfather was reasonably angry and hurt when he discovered the girl he was dating cheated on him with his brother, Michael, and he disappeared. The family had no idea where he went, and after many months with no word or sighting, they began to think he was dead. Michael married that girl, but through the years, he continued searching for my grandfather, with no luck.

"Michael and Mary had three children, and Aileen, whom I met today, was the youngest. She'd promised her father when he was dying that she'd keep searching for my grandfather. She'd been praying she'd find out what happened to him before she died. She's almost one hundred, so she was starting to run out of time." Bruce let out a small chuckle.

"Your poor grandfather!"

"Yes. He must have been devastated to leave his family and country and never return. But he never said anything about any of it. Well, not that I can remember."

The waitress returned with their cups of tea and asked if they were ready to order.

"Can we have a few more minutes?" Bruce asked.

"Sure. No problem." She smiled and stepped away.

"I'm sorry. I got carried away." He picked up his menu but only gave it a cursory glance.

"It's okay. I can see how pleased you are to have found some information…even if it was sad," Wendy said.

"Yes, it was wonderful. And it seems I come from a large family."

Wendy chuckled, her eyes twinkling. "A big Irish family? Really? Now, that's unusual."

Bruce tilted his head. Was she making fun of him?

Wendy shook her head and laughed. "I'm joking."

"Oh." Bruce's shoulders slumped. "Sorry. Sometimes I'm as slow as molasses."

She sobered. "I apologize. Maybe I shouldn't joke with people I don't know."

Bruce smiled, realizing she was being her authentic self. "No, don't stop. I find you interesting, joking and all." Their gazes met and held, and his heart picked up its pace, same as when they had coffee together that morning. It was the first time he'd felt a strong physical and emotional attraction to a lady since Faith. But what could come of it? Nothing. She'd return to her life in Sydney, and he'd return to his life in Texas. But even so, it was nice being in her company. He'd enjoy this evening getting to know her, and not think any further than that.

Wendy's cheeks grew pink. She lowered her gaze and focused on the menu. He shouldn't have been so forward. Now he'd made her uncomfortable.

Fortunately, the waitress returned to take their orders.

"I...I think I'll have the steak and ale pie," Wendy said without looking up.

"And I'll have the rabbit stew." It was the first item on the menu he saw when he glanced down.

After the waitress left, they both quietly sipped their tea and the awkward moment passed.

"Are you going to meet the rest of the family?" Wendy asked in a soft voice.

Bruce set his cup down and looked up. "Yes. Aileen's invited me back the day after tomorrow to meet as many as she can get together at short notice."

"I'm so happy for you. That's wonderful!"

"Thank you." He smiled, lowered his gaze again, and wrapped his hands around his cup as an idea formulated in his head. But did he dare? They barely knew each other, but she was like a breath of fresh air. Maybe he should risk it. Be daring. Drawing a steadying breath, he lifted his gaze and met hers again. "You wouldn't like to come with me, would you?"

Her eyes widened, almost in shock. A small breath blew from his mouth. He'd done it again. What was it about this woman that made him so forward? It wasn't like him at all. He hadn't taken much of an interest in dating in the years Faith had been gone. But there was something special about Wendy.

"That's lovely of you to ask, but I'm leaving on that tour the day after tomorrow," she replied apologetically.

"Oh, that's right." Disappointment filled him and weighed him down like a lead balloon. Over coffee that morning, she'd told him about the five-day tour of Northern Ireland she was taking before she flew to London, but he'd forgotten.

"Otherwise I would have loved to go with you," she continued.

He blinked. "Really?"

She nodded, her mouth curving into the most beautiful of smiles. "Yes."

His heart soared momentarily—it was such bad timing. If only they'd met earlier.

The waitress arrived with their meals, and once she left, he asked if he could give thanks.

Wendy smiled sweetly, her brown eyes soft and warm. "Of

course." She bowed her head and he did the same, pausing a moment to settle his heart before he prayed. He was tempted to take her hand as they did at home when they gave thanks, but he refrained—it would be too brazen. He steadied himself and then prayed, "Heavenly Father, thank You for Your abundant blessings. Thank You for the great company, and thank You for this good food. In Jesus' name. Amen."

"Amen," Wendy repeated.

They began to eat, and he told her more about the family he'd just discovered. Halfway through the meal, he realized he'd been talking nonstop and that Wendy had grown quiet. He put down his silverware and apologized. "Are you all right?"

"I'm fine, thanks for asking. I'm just concerned about my youngest daughter, that's all. She's been on my mind all day. She rang this morning when I was waiting for the bus and I said I'd call her back, but I haven't had a chance."

"Is she in trouble?"

"Not really, but her boyfriend dumped her and she got drunk. I'm worried for her."

"Oh." Bruce blinked. He hadn't expected that.

Wendy let out a heavy sigh as a wistful look crossed her face. "She gets drunk often."

"That's not good."

"No, it's not. I pray for her constantly, but I'm concerned she's going to do something stupid." Wendy's love and concern for her daughter was evident in her tone, and Bruce's heart went out to her.

"It must be a constant worry," he said.

"It is. And it's so hard not to compare her to my eldest. I try not to, but Natalie's so sensible, and Paige is so... so..."

"Troubled?"

"Yes." Wendy nibbled her bottom lip, but a look of relief reflected in her eyes. "She's never gotten over her father dying. How did you know?"

He shrugged. "I guessed. My wife died ten years ago, and my Aiden was like that. He took his mother's passing badly. Not that any of us coped well with it. It was such a shock."

"I'm so sorry. How's your son now?"

"Much better, but Andrew, my middle son, well, that's a different matter." Bruce paused. He preferred not talking about Andrew, so he changed the subject. "Is there anyone you can call to check on your daughter?"

"Yes. I was thinking I'd call Natalie when I get in tonight."

"Good idea. It might ease your mind."

Wendy nodded. "I think you're right. Thanks for understanding."

Without thinking, he reached out and took her hand, stroking her soft skin with his thumb. "We've experienced similar things, you and I. I know how you're feeling."

She didn't withdraw her hand, and he gulped when she gripped his tighter. Their gazes locked and he knew then, that after just a few short hours spent with this wonderful woman, falling in love again was a real possibility.

49

$\mathcal{T}$he tour guide cleared her voice and called everyone to attention before checking the passenger list and asking people to find a seat.

Without thinking, Bruce almost placed his hand on the small of Wendy's back as they joined the line. He stopped himself just in time. It seemed such a natural thing to do, but it would have been too presumptuous. But then, would it? On their way home after supper the evening before, she'd asked him to join her today on the day tour to the Cliffs of Moher on the west coast, and he was hopeful that she felt the same way he did. There was a spark, a very strong spark, a connection he thought he'd never feel with any other woman but Faith, and he wanted to explore it further.

They sat next to each other on the coach and made easy conversation. Arriving at the cliffs, which rose slowly from the town of Doolin, and, according to the tour guide, ascended to over seven hundred feet and stretched south for nearly five miles to Hags Head, he offered his hand to help her down the steps. Not that she needed help, but he was old-fashioned that way. They'd been warned about the icy winds that could whip off the Atlantic over the rugged coastline even in the height of summer, so given it was Autumn, they'd come prepared and wore gloves, but the mere touch of her hand in his sent a warming shiver through him.

They strolled together along the walkway, pausing to take photos of the cliffs and occasionally of each other. One of the other tourists offered to take a photo of them together using their phone cameras. They laughed, said they weren't a couple, but accepted anyway.

"Our children are going to ask questions when they see these photos." Wendy met his gaze and laughed again.

He threw his head back and let out a huge chuckle. "Let them ask."

"Don't you worry about what they'll think?" Wendy asked, turning serious.

"Not really. We're adults, and we're not doing anything wrong. Shall we sit?" He gestured to the wooden bench just behind them.

Wendy smiled and nodded, and without thinking, he placed his hand in hers. Once seated, he kept hold of her hand and gazed out at the endless sea. Salty wind whipped his face. "My wife, Faith, died ten years ago." He closed his eyes. Sometimes, it seemed like yesterday that he'd gotten that knock on the door, and the ranger told him that Faith had died in a wreck. He'd never forget it, and he'd never forget the love they shared. But she was gone, and now he was here, sitting on top of a cliff on the rugged Irish coastline with a wonderful woman. He drew a deep breath and turned to her. "And last year, I had cancer."

Wendy's eyes widened. She squeezed his hand. "No!"

He nodded. "Bowel cancer."

"You obviously beat it..."

"Yep, the doctors are confident they got it all." His voice trailed off and they both sat in silence. He stroked her hand. "When I was ill, I realized that life isn't a rehearsal and I wanted to start living again, which was why I booked this trip." He squeezed her hand, turned to look into her face, and held his gaze steady. "Meeting you has been unexpected and thrilling. I truly feel a connection." Was he being too upfront? Had he jumped the gun? But he was an honest man and he liked Wendy way too much to play games.

She lowered her gaze and remained still and quiet. Too quiet. He'd spoken too soon. His spirits sank and he released a disappointed breath. Maybe he'd misread her, and she didn't reciprocate his feelings.

Finally, she lifted her gaze and looked deep into his eyes.

He held his breath.

"I...I know what you mean. I feel that way too." She paused, let out a slow breath.

His pulse raced. Had he heard correctly? She felt the same?

"But I'm leaving for my tour tomorrow." She shrugged. "Where does that leave us?"

Relief flooded and overwhelmed him. He thought quickly. "I'll be in London in just over a week. Can we meet up then?"

A broad smile grew on her beautiful face, warming his heart. "I'd love to."

They remained seated on the bench in comfortable silence

as seagulls squawked and circled overhead and wind bit their faces. He slipped his arm around her shoulder and pulled her close. It felt so right.

Soon after, they strolled along the path that hugged the top of the cliffs. Reaching some steps, they headed down and discovered a quaint old pub. The landlord of the 'The Smugglers Inn' greeted them with a big, gap-toothed smile. They had difficulty understanding him but managed to glean that the Irish stew was very tasty and ordered two bowls.

When the stew arrived, Bruce gave thanks for the meal, this time holding Wendy's hand as he prayed.

"This is delicious," she remarked after taking her first mouthful. The stew was indeed good and just what they needed to warm their stomachs on a blustery Irish day at the cliffs.

Bruce nodded. "It is. My grandfather sometimes made stew, but it never tasted like this." He chuckled as he recalled the large pot that often bubbled on the range back home at the ranch. At the time, Bruce wasn't impressed with the simple meal and he often looked at the pot with dread, knowing he wouldn't be allowed to leave the table until every drop in his bowl had been consumed. He took another spoonful, savoring the taste of the hearty stew as it slid easily down his throat.

Wendy laughed. "Was your grandfather's stew really that bad?"

Bruce pulled a wry face and nodded. "I'm afraid it was, but this meal has restored my faith in it."

They continued eating and chatting. He wanted to ask Wendy to dine with him again that evening but was concerned she might consider it too much, too soon, so he hesitated. But he decided to ask anyway—life was too short and precious for regret. Setting down his fork, he wiped his mouth with his napkin and lifted his gaze to hers. "Wendy, would you have supper with me again tonight?"

He knew immediately by the expression on her face what her answer would be. How was it possible to be so disappointed when they'd only known each other such a short time?

"I'm sorry, but do you mind if I take a rain check? I'm a little tired and I need to be ready for tomorrow."

"Of course. I should have realized. I'm sorry."

She squeezed his hand. "It's okay. We'll have plenty of time together in London."

He gazed into her warm eyes, and although he didn't want to let her out of his sight, he took comfort knowing they'd meet again in London.

CHAPTER 7

*W*endy studied her reflection in the mirror. She wasn't vain, but she wanted to look her best for her goodbye with Bruce. Although she'd declined dinner with him the previous evening, her thoughts had turned to him often during the night as she prepared for her tour of Northern Ireland. The silver-haired Texan had certainly captured her heart in the few short days they'd known each other, but she wavered between giddiness and sensibility. Had she been acting irresponsibly? Holding hands with a man she barely knew? What would Greg think? *What would her children think?* But she couldn't ignore the flutters in her heart each time she thought of him. Flutters she hadn't felt since she and Greg had started dating all those years ago.

Dressed casually in jeans, boots, and a warm argyle sweater, Wendy applied a dash of pink lipstick, the only colour her honey-brown skin needed. She called a porter for her luggage and followed him down to reception to settle her bill.

Although she hadn't dined with Bruce the previous evening, they'd eaten a quick breakfast together, and he'd promised to meet her in the foyer and wait with her until the coach left. Arriving downstairs, she joined the line of people checking in and out, but by the time she managed to get away from the reception desk, the coach was already waiting.

"I'm so sorry," she said as she approached Bruce. He'd been standing to one side waiting, and she'd been very conscious of his presence, and his gaze on her back.

"It's fine, Wendy. Until we meet again..." He placed his hands lightly on her arms and gazed into her eyes. Her heart pounded. He sounded jovial, but she could see that their parting was as difficult for him as it was for her.

Without thinking, she stepped into his arms. Resting her head against his chest, she closed her eyes and did her best to enjoy the moment and ignore the conflicting emotions bouncing around in her heart. After sharing a hug, she stood on tiptoe and gently kissed his cheek. "Until London." She smiled and then quickly stepped away before she changed her mind and decided to stay.

She made her way up the steps of the coach, and once seated, waved, swallowing the lump in her throat as the coach began moving down the bustling street. It wasn't long before Bruce became a pin prick in the distance.

Drawing a steadying breath, Wendy settled in her seat and turned her thoughts to the tour. The first stop was Belfast, where she'd spend two days and two nights. The journey was just over one-hundred miles and was scheduled to take nearly three hours. She was pleased it would take that long because she needed time to think about Bruce and her growing feelings. She felt comfortable with him, but how would Simon and Paige react if she told them she was seeing someone? Not that she and Bruce were seeing each other and dating. They were just friends, but she sensed it could grow to something more if she allowed it. How would Paige cope with a new man in her mother's life? Just the night before, she'd called again, drunk, berating the God who'd snatched her father from her.

Wendy closed her eyes and prayed again for her youngest daughter. *Heavenly Father, please watch over Paige. Let her see how much You love and care for her, and help her to know that You only want the best for her. Please draw her to Yourself.* Wendy paused, gulped. *"And Heavenly Father, please guide me with regards to Bruce. Thank You for bringing us together, but please show me what I should do as I don't want to make decisions that will have a negative impact on my family. In Jesus' precious name. Amen.*

"Are you okay, love?" the woman beside her asked in a broad English accent.

Wendy blinked and opened her eyes. So preoccupied with Bruce and Paige, she'd only given a nod to the woman when she'd sat in the seat beside her. Wendy now studied the woman as she smiled. About sixty, she had an open and honest face, and Wendy instantly warmed to her. "Yes, I'm fine, thanks for asking." She held out her hand. "I'm Wendy."

"I'm Jean," the woman replied. She instantly began talking about her family and the reasons why she was on the trip. By the time they arrived at the hotel in Belfast they were firm friends and had decided to enjoy the tour in each other's company. Wendy liked Jean—she took her mind off Bruce and her children, although she'd also shared a little about her family with her. But only the good bits.

Wendy loved the days spent in Belfast and the trip to the Giants Causeway, which was stunning and took her breath away. She revelled in the history of it all, seeing what she'd read about and taught her students for so many years coming to life in front of her very eyes, but something was lacking. Jean was a wonderful travelling companion, but Wendy couldn't help but think how much more enjoyable it might have been had she shared the experience with Bruce. All the while, she was counting down the days until she saw him again in London.

DUBLIN LOST its charm for Bruce after Wendy left. He missed their casual meals, their conversation, and their prayers of thanks. Although he didn't know her well, they'd connected, and that connection had started with their mutual love of the Lord. They shared similar morals, enjoyed the same things, and without her companionship, his joy in discovering Ireland and his long-lost family had diminished significantly.

Bruce looked at his reflection and decided that the fresh Irish air agreed with him. He'd looked gaunt and weak since his chemotherapy had stopped several months before, but since coming to Ireland, his color had returned and his face had filled out. He looked better than he had for a very long time, and that pleased him. And it would please his sons, too. He quickly picked up his phone, took a selfie, and sent it off with a message to each of them. Within seconds, his phone rang and he chuckled. Of course it would be Nate. "Hi son, how you doin'?"

"I'm great. And wow, you look better!" Nate exclaimed.

"That'll be the Irish air...that be." Bruce replied in the worst Irish accent imaginable. They both laughed.

"You look healthy and happy." Nate's voice grew serious. "I was wrong to try stopping you from going, I can see that now."

Bruce smiled. His son was stubborn, but his heart was in the right place, and if he knew he was in the wrong, he'd be the first to admit it. Bruce thought about the arguments he'd had with Nate over this trip, and deciding not to mention them, simply said, "That's fine son, no harm done. It's all in the past now."

"So, you're going to meet the clan this evening?" Nate asked.

"Yes, my cousin Aileen arranged it. I think it's goin' to be quite an experience." Bruce chuckled as he thought of his elderly cousin. He continued talking for a few more moments before ending the call. Checking his phone, Bruce noticed a message from Aiden, which simply read: *Looking good, Dad. God Bless.* No response from Andrew, but he knew there wouldn't be, and with a deep sigh, slipped his phone into his pocket and went downstairs to try to fill his day without Wendy.

Later that day, Bruce made his way to Aileen's house. He enjoyed meeting his relatives, but there were so many of them and the faces and names became a blur as he was introduced to one cousin after another. Although he couldn't remember their individual names, he was sure he'd never met a friendlier group of people in his entire life. He also couldn't stop wondering how different it would have been if Wendy had come.

When the room cleared and almost all the guests had said

their goodbyes, he sat in the fireside chair and closed his eyes briefly as a wave of tiredness swept over him.

"Penny for yer thoughts, me lad."

He opened his eyes and straightened. Aileen stood next to the chair with a steaming hot cup of tea in her hand. She passed it to him and then shuffled back to sit in her favorite, hard-backed chair beside the dining table. "Well?" she added as she made herself comfortable.

Bruce pondered her question. He hadn't told anyone about his growing feelings toward Wendy, but he felt the need to tell someone. Maybe Aileen would have some opinion about whether he was crazy or not to be falling for a woman who lived halfway around the world and whom he'd only just met.

He drew a breath and embarked on the story of how he'd accidentally spilled coffee on this wonderful woman, and that although they'd only known each other a few days, how she'd captured his heart and consumed his thoughts. "You think I'm crazy!" he finally said as he leaned back in the chair.

Aileen's eyes twinkled. "Love is often crazy, lad. She sounds like a lovely lass, and I'd say, go for it."

Bruce's eyes widened; he hadn't expected that.

She continued. "We're lucky if we find true love once in our lives. To find it twice is a blessing from the Heavenly Father Himself, so grab that blessing with both hands, my boy, because it might not come along again."

Bruce considered her words while sipping his tea. Strangely, his muddled thoughts about Wendy began to settle, and he liked the idea that his feelings for her were a gift from the Father. He also knew he must trust God to guide them, because if his relationship with Wendy developed, no doubt plenty of challenges lay ahead.

He stayed with Aileen a while longer and helped clean up, but when she began to slow, he knew he needed to take his leave so she could retire, although he could have happily talked with his cousin all night, such was her wisdom and wit.

He visited several more times over the following days, but when it came time to bid goodbye for the last time, Bruce was surprised to discover himself growing teary. He'd built a quick rapport with Aileen, and it was unlikely they'd see each other again this side of heaven. Her age was against them, but he also knew that he'd remember her and her warm welcome for the rest of his life.

"I'll be leaving then," he said as he pulled on his coat. Aileen had called a taxi cab and it had just arrived and was waiting outside.

"Aye, take care of yourself, me lad," she answered with a sniffle.

"You too...it's been lovely getting to know you..." Bruce searched for more eloquent words to express how he felt, but his tongue had stilled and his brain had stopped working.

"I know, I know," Aileen whispered softly. "Likewise, lad, likewise." She then pushed him toward the door. "That taxi cab will be costing you a fortune."

Bruce chuckled as he climbed into the back seat. His last memory of his cousin was of her toothless, but adorable grin as she stood on her porch and waved as the taxi drove away.

CHAPTER 8

 ondon

WENDY WOKE with a smile on her face, a rarity over the years since Greg's passing. Although she knew it was ridiculous for a woman of her age to feel so giddy at the prospect of meeting up with a man she'd only known such a short time, the prolonged anticipation of her reunion with Bruce was almost unbearable.

In him, she felt she'd found a kindred spirit, someone who understood the pain and grief of losing a spouse, who cared deeply for his adult children, and who also shared her faith. In many ways, it felt like she'd known him forever, and yet, sometimes it seemed just yesterday that he'd spilled that coffee on her. It was the same feeling she'd experienced when she first met Greg, but she was younger then, a lot younger. It surprised her that this kind of thing happened to women of her vintage. Not that she was old, but she'd never thought she'd know the wonderful feelings of blossoming love again.

They'd texted each other over the last few days and the magic of their budding romance became apparent through their words. She waited with heightened anticipation for the ping of her phone signalling the arrival of one of his texts, and although his words weren't overly eloquent or complicated, they were heartfelt and enough to make her heart race. For the first time in such a very long time, she felt enjoyment in the now, and excited about the future. She'd thought those feelings were gone from her life for good, and thanked her Heavenly Father they weren't.

Stepping onto the tiny balcony, she inhaled a lungful of London air. Car fumes mingled with pungent spices wafting from the Indian restaurant on the opposite side of the road. A heavy fog clung like a blanket over the city, but below, London was waking. A black cab broke from the traffic and stopped in front of the hotel, picking up a male passenger who seemed impatient to be going somewhere. Most likely the airport since he had a suitcase with him.

How she loved the bustling city. Wendy bit her lip as the memories of the time spent there with Greg threatened to weigh her down. Her buoyant mood faded. Was it foolish thinking she could find love again? Bruce was so different to Greg, and they lived so far from each other. How could it ever work? *Lord, please give me wisdom and clarity. And please stop me if I'm being foolish.*

Drawing a slow breath, she turned and walked back into the hotel room, shutting the traffic noise out as she closed the door. That morning she'd arranged to visit Greg's grandmother, Elizabeth Miller. Wendy expected it to be an emotional meeting—they hadn't seen each other since Greg's passing, but she hoped they could move on quickly so their meeting at the party the following afternoon could be a joyous affair, filled with celebration, just as it should be. For now, she'd try to forget about her quandary with Bruce and give Elizabeth Miller all the attention she deserved.

GREG'S GRANDMOTHER still lived in the same stately manor home on the southern outskirts of London that she'd lived in all her married life. Arriving in a taxi at the appointed hour of ten o'clock, Wendy steeled herself and quietly prayed for strength. Not so much for her meeting with Elizabeth—she was looking forward to that. She knew that all the memories of the year she and Greg lived here would be revived. Precious memories that would tear at her heart and make his absence more real, and for that, she needed strength. But she'd come half-way around the world to attend his grandmother's party, so she needed to face the memories head-on.

She paid the taxi driver and climbed out, stepping onto gravel that crunched underfoot. Pulling her coat tighter, she crossed the path and paused beneath the portico. How many times had Greg stolen a kiss from her in this very spot before they went inside? She smiled at the memory, and then drew a steadying breath and pressed the buzzer.

Elizabeth must have been hovering nearby, because just moments later, the door opened and the genteel old woman stood before her, just a little more stooped than the last time

Wendy had seen her almost twenty years previously. Even at the grand old age of ninety, glimpses of Elizabeth's beauty were still visible. Her face had aged, but her perfect bone structure remained, and coupled with her high cheek bones, gave her an almost regal appearance. Her hair was snowy white, and her skin, although pale and wrinkled, glowed softly. Her bright blue eyes still danced merrily and Wendy guessed, still didn't miss a thing.

Her wrinkled face broke into a broad smile. "Wendy! My dear girl, come in, come in."

Wendy stepped inside and gave the elderly woman a big hug, pushing back the tears that threatened to fall. "Elizabeth, it's so wonderful to see you." She wiped her eyes and smiled into Elizabeth's.

"And you, dear girl. It's been too long."

"Yes, it has." Wendy linked her arm in Elizabeth's and walked slowly with her to the lounge, where Elizabeth motioned for her to sit in a chair facing hers.

"I've asked Maria to bring some tea," Elizabeth said.

"Maria?"

"My live-in help."

"Oh. I didn't know you had help, but I'm pleased. She must be company for you, too," Wendy said.

"Yes, she's a real sweetie. Looks after me like I'm royalty." Elizabeth's eyes twinkled as she settled into her chair.

"Greg and I often used to think you were."

Their gazes met, and the years slipped away. Elizabeth reached out and took Wendy's hand. "How are you coping, dear? I was so sorry to hear about Greg's passing."

Wendy inhaled slowly. "I won't say it's been easy, but you'd know what it's like." Greg's grandfather, William Miller, had died in his early sixties, leaving Elizabeth a widow in her late fifties, just like Wendy.

A faraway look came over Elizabeth's face. "Yes, I do. It was such a hard and lonely time."

"You never thought about remarrying?" Wendy asked tentatively.

"No. Although I came close once."

Wendy leaned forward. "Really?"

"You didn't know?"

Wendy shook her head. "No. Would you tell me about it?"

Elizabeth must have wondered at Wendy's interest, but just then, a young woman whom Wendy assumed was Maria, pushed the door open and entered, carrying a tray laden with a teapot, two dainty china cups and saucers, and a plate of freshly cooked scones that smelled divine. She set the tray on the small table between the chairs. "Would you like me to pour, Mrs. Miller?" she asked.

Wendy's head jerked that direction. Was Maria asking her the question? Then she laughed at herself. There were two Mrs. Millers in the room.

Elizabeth held her hand out, took Maria's, and smiled. "No, we'll be fine, thank you, but Maria, meet my grandson's wife, Wendy. She's come all the way from Australia to attend my party."

Maria wasn't much older than Paige, but unlike Wendy's daughter, the live-in help had a jolly face and a pleasant smile. She gave a small curtsy as she said hello in a quiet, sweet voice.

Wendy smiled. "It's nice to meet you, Maria. I'm so glad you're caring for Elizabeth. She's such a dear lady."

The girl blushed. "Thank you. It's nice to meet you, too." She turned to Elizabeth. "Is there anything else I can get you?"

"No, that's all for now, thank you," Elizabeth replied in a kindly voice.

Maria nodded and made a hasty exit.

Elizabeth gazed after her. "She's such a sweet thing, but so self-effacing. Not a grain of confidence when she first came."

Wendy was about to say she still didn't have any, but refrained. They obviously got on well, and she didn't want to say anything that would upset Greg's grandmother. Instead, she offered to pour.

"Perfect. And I'll look after my scone." Elizabeth chuckled lightly as she lathered the plump scone with jam and cream and then proceeded to take a mouthful.

Wendy laughed to herself. She now knew where Greg and Natalie got their appetites from.

Wiping her face, Elizabeth picked up their previous conversation. "James was the brother of a close friend, and we'd known each other for years. He lost his wife about the same time that I lost William, and we helped each other through our time of grief. But he wanted more. I didn't. William and I had such a wonderful marriage and I just couldn't bring myself to marry anyone else." She paused and met Wendy's gaze. "But that doesn't mean you shouldn't."

Wendy gulped, almost spurting tea from her mouth. Was her quandary that obvious? She quickly composed herself, but not before Elizabeth raised a finely plucked brow.

"So, there is someone…" An amused grin grew on her face. "I thought there might be."

Wendy chuckled. Elizabeth had always been astute. How

could she have forgotten? She set her teacup down, took a breath and began to tell Elizabeth all about Bruce.

"He sounds wonderful. A Texan? I don't think I've met one of them in real life. Invite him to the party. I'd like to meet him."

Wendy blinked. "Are you sure?"

"Of course. I wouldn't have said so otherwise."

"Okay. I will. Thank you." Wendy smiled as her mind whirled. She hadn't considered inviting Bruce to the party.

Elizabeth picked up her cup and sipped her tea. "You're welcome. Now, tell me about your family. How are they all? Natalie, Simon, and..." She hesitated, obviously struggling to recall Paige's name. Not surprising since she had more than twenty great-grandchildren at last count.

Wendy helped her out. "Paige."

"Yes, of course. How could I forget?"

"You have so many to remember, and besides, she was only a baby when you last saw her." Warm memories of the family's trip to celebrate Christmas with their English family when the children were young made her nostalgic again. But she hadn't answered Elizabeth's question.

She took another deep breath. It was easy to tell her about Natalie and the upcoming wedding, but harder to be honest about Paige and Simon and their challenges. But in the end, she did. They were Elizabeth's great-grandchildren, after all, and Wendy had a sneaking suspicion that nothing would surprise the elderly woman.

Elizabeth patted her hand when she finished. "I worried about two of my children as well. Stay strong, Wendy. Pray for them. Trust God to do the work in their hearts, but accept that they have free will and might not choose to submit to Him, despite your prayers."

Wendy guessed that Elizabeth was referring to Graham, Greg's uncle, who'd announced he was a homosexual at age forty, sending shock waves through the family. He'd died of AIDS not long before Greg passed away.

Elizabeth continued. "But nothing will stop us from loving and caring for them. They're our children, and just like God loves us unconditionally, we should also love them unconditionally. Even if we don't like their choices." Her eyes filled.

Wendy squeezed the older woman's frail hand gently. "It's not easy being a parent, is it?"

"No, not even at my age. But I wouldn't trade it for anything."

"Me either." And Wendy wouldn't. Her children were her life, and she loved each of them dearly.

Elizabeth dabbed her eyes with a tissue. "They make us who we are. We learn from them, and we grow stronger because we have to, but most of all, they bring us great joy." She paused and let out the tiniest of chuckles. "Most of the time."

"You're absolutely right," Wendy said. She needed to remember that when Simon and Paige's behaviour dragged her down and despair filled her heart.

"I'm sorry I've given you a sermon, dear. I'm sure you didn't expect one when you came to visit."

Wendy smiled at the wise, old lady. "No, but it was what I needed."

They continued chatting and time passed until Wendy glanced at her watch. Midday...Bruce's plane would have landed. Her heart began to beat with anticipation. "I need to go, I'm so sorry," she said, quickly gathering her belongings.

"That's perfectly fine, dear. It's been wonderful spending time with you. Just make sure you bring that cowboy with you tomorrow." Elizabeth's blue eyes flashed with a mischievous twinkle.

"If you insist," Wendy said with a laugh.

They bid each other good-bye, and Wendy called a cab to take her back to her hotel. With so many thoughts whirling in her head, she needed some down time before Bruce arrived, but she was unlikely to get much. The traffic was thick and slow, and as the taxi driver weaved in and out of the London traffic, Wendy used the time to re-commit her children, her life, and her relationships to God. Especially one with a certain cowboy. And she thanked Him for the time she'd spent with Elizabeth. A wise woman who'd experienced both great joy and heartache in her ninety years, and whom God had used to give Wendy encouragement when she needed it the most.

Arriving back at the Hotel Alba in Paddington, a four-star hotel close to Marble Arch, Oxford Street, and just a two minute walk from Hyde Park, she had just enough time to freshen up before heading down to the foyer to wait for Bruce. He'd booked a room in the hotel and was catching the hotel's complimentary shuttle from the airport.

With the shuttle due to arrive any moment, Wendy sat in one of the oversized armchairs and waited.

SEATED in the front seat of the hotel's shuttle bus, Bruce took in the sights of London as the bus weaved its way slowly through the traffic. It was his first visit to the city, and he was looking forward to exploring it, but even more so, he looked forward to exploring it with Wendy. *Wendy...* His heart rate kicked up a notch. Would it still be the same as it had been in Dublin? They'd gotten on so well, but during the week they'd been apart, he'd occasionally wondered if he'd been acting like a foolish old man. Maybe it was one of those holiday romances that seemed wonderful at the time, but in the clear light of day, was destined to fail. He did his best to push those thoughts aside as the bus stopped in front of the Hotel Alba. He prayed it wouldn't be like that, because he'd fallen head over heels in love with her.

His hands shook as he took hold of the rail and carefully navigated the stairs of the bus. He half expected to see her standing on the sidewalk waiting for him. He looked around, but she wasn't there, and disappointment filled him. Maybe she'd changed her mind. He waited anxiously on the sidewalk while the driver pulled bags from the luggage compartment underneath the bus.

When his bag emerged, he thanked the driver and turned around to head into the hotel. He stopped in his tracks. Wendy was walking toward him. His heart skipped a beat when she lifted a hand and waved. She looked beautiful. Her light brown hair bounced softly on her shoulders, and her face held a smile that warmed his heart. She was dressed in a simple, knee-length, blue dress which looked wonderful on her. Setting his bag on the ground, he approached her and gazed deeply into her eyes. He so wanted to hug her, but something stopped him. Moments passed, and then he couldn't help himself—he wrapped his arms around her, held her close, and placed a gentle kiss on her cheek. "It's so good to see you, Wendy," he whispered into her ear. Her hair smelled of fresh flowers, and her soft curves molded into the contours of his body like a well-fitting glove.

She drew back and smiled into his eyes. "It's good to see you too, Bruce." Their gazes locked, and he knew what he'd felt in Dublin wasn't just a holiday romance.

"Come inside. You must be tired after the flight," she said.

He wasn't. Seeing her had heightened all his senses and he was fully awake, but he walked in with her, anyway. "It's a lovely hotel," he said, more to make small talk than anything else as they approached the reception desk. Wendy stood beside him as he checked in. The young woman was pleasant, her accent very English, making his Texan drawl as obvious as an elephant in the room.

"The porter will take your bag to your room. Enjoy your stay, Mr. McCarthy." She smiled as she handed him the key.

"Thank you, I'm sure I will." Bruce tipped his hat and stepped away. When he met Wendy's gaze, he grinned and squeezed her hand. "Let me freshen up and then perhaps we can take a stroll?"

She smiled. "I'd like that."

"Shall we meet here in half an hour?"

"Sounds perfect. I'll sit here and wait," she answered.

"Are you sure?"

"Yes. I've got my book, and I'll grab a cup of tea."

"I'll be as quick as I can." Without hesitation, he leaned forward and popped another kiss on her cheek.

CHAPTER 9

endy couldn't concentrate on her book. How could she? Bruce was here... Her breath had caught when she saw him alight from the shuttle bus. Unmissable in his jeans, boots and cowboy hat, her heart had fluttered so much she thought she would have a heart attack. The feelings were so foreign after all this time, but all of a sudden, she felt alive again.

She closed her book and sipped her tea, keeping an eye on the lift. Several times it opened, and finally, Bruce stepped out. She lifted her hand to wave to him, but there was no need— he'd seen her and was already walking towards her.

He sat beside her and smiled. "I brought you something."

"Really?"

He nodded and held out a neatly wrapped box with a green bow on top.

Heavier than expected, she placed the box on her lap. What could it be? She began unwrapping it, and inside found a box of Irish Fudge. She lifted her gaze and smiled. "Thank you. This looks scrumptious."

"Made lovingly by my cousin. Aileen insisted I bring it for you."

"How thoughtful of her! Would you like a piece?" Wendy held the box to him.

He laughed while rubbing his stomach. "I think I've eaten more than my fair share already, but go on, you have one."

"I think I will." She'd already put all thoughts of her mother-of the-bride dress to the back of her mind. When she got home, she'd go on a crash diet. Hopefully there'd be enough time to take off the weight she'd put on while travelling. She took a small square from the box and slipped it into her mouth, where it promptly began melting. "Delicious!" she managed to say between chews. "Are you sure you don't want one?" She offered the box again.

"Oh, why not?" Bruce laughed and slipped a piece into his mouth.

Moments passed while they devoured the tasty, sweet fudge. "Shall we head out?" he finally asked.

"Yes. Where would you like to go?"

"I have no idea. Be my tour guide."

She laughed. "Okay. Let's go."

After slipping the box into her purse, they headed out onto the busy street and soon found themselves in Hyde Park. The setting was peaceful, allowing them time to talk and enjoy each other's company. There'd be time to explore the buildings and tourist spots later.

Bruce told her about the days he'd spent in Dublin after she left, and she told him about her tour of Northern Ireland. It was small talk—neither really saying what was on their hearts, but how could they? It was too soon, and they had a whole week to spend together. Wendy had to keep pinching herself to make sure that strolling through Hyde Park with a handsome cowboy was really happening.

"Shall we get something to eat?" Bruce asked after they ambled down The Broad Walk past Kensington Palace and emerged onto Kensington Road.

"I know just the place!" Wendy said. "Follow me!"

"Sounds intriguing." He increased his pace to keep up with her. "Where are you taking me?"

"Wait and see," she replied, winking.

They headed down Kensington Road, past the Royal Albert Hall. "I'd like to take you there one evening," he said.

Wendy swallowed the lump that rose in her throat. One of her best memories was of the evening she and Greg had seen Luciano Pavarotti perform at the Hall. But that was so long ago, and this was now. She squeezed Bruce's hand and replied, "I would enjoy that very much."

They crossed Exhibition Road. "There are quite a few museums down there. Maybe we could explore them one day," she said.

"Which museums?"

"Oh, the Natural History Museum, the Science Museum, and the Victoria and Albert Museum, plus there are some lovely gardens."

"You've been to them before?"

She nodded. "Yes. I used to go often during the year we lived here." How many hours had she spent looking through the various exhibits while Greg was at work?

"Oh. I'm sorry."

"It's okay, really."

They turned right down Trevor Place, skirted around the Square of the same name, and emerged in front of Harrods.

Bruce laughed. "Of course!"

Wendy flashed him a smile. "My favourite place in all of London!" They entered the store and sauntered past counters of perfume and jewellery. Finally, Wendy guided him to the Tea Rooms. "Let me introduce you to 'English Tea'."

They chose a table tucked in a quiet corner and sat opposite each other. She ordered a pot of English Afternoon Tea, scones with clotted cream and strawberry jam, and a plate of cucumber sandwiches.

While they waited, Bruce reached his hand across the table and took hers. Her heart raced as his thumb gently massaged the top of her hand.

"I missed you, Wendy. Dublin wasn't the same after you left."

She lifted her gaze and met his. This was like a dream. How could she be sitting in Harrods taking tea and holding this dear man's hand? Her thumping heart told her it was real. "Oh Bruce, what are we doing?"

"We're falling in love, that's what we're doing."

"But how can it work?"

"I don't know, my sweet girl, but let's not worry about that right now. Let's just enjoy our time together and see what happens. I've learned to take one day at a time, and to let tomorrow look after itself."

"I wish I could do that."

"It takes practice, but it's worth the effort."

A waitress wearing a white ruffled apron delivered their afternoon tea, which was more like a meal than a snack.

"Where do I start?" he asked.

"You can pour." She smiled at the man who'd already captured her heart and sensed she was about to be swept off her feet. She prayed neither of them would get hurt.

"My pleasure, my darlin'."

She chuckled as he lifted the teapot and began to pour. The tea was delicious, just as she remembered. Strong and sweet, with a hint of exotic spice, and the scones and sandwiches were tasty and fresh. But it was the company that made the afternoon so special as she and Bruce discussed so many topics. By the time they left, Wendy felt like she knew almost everything about him, even that he vehemently disliked peas, which she couldn't quite understand, since peas were one of her favourite vegetables.

Afterwards, they spent more time walking around the department store. Wendy chose some gorgeous, but small gifts of handmade soaps for her children and a few of her friends back home. Bruce did the same. They decided to catch a taxi back to the hotel, and to take a rest in their rooms before meeting for dinner that evening.

As the lift opened at Wendy's floor in the hotel, Bruce squeezed her hand and smiled. "Until tonight." He leaned in and kissed her cheek, his lips soft and warm on her skin, and the lingering scent of tea sweet on his breath.

When she stepped out on her own and walked down the hallway to her room, Wendy couldn't wipe the smile from her face. Until she looked at the phone and saw ten missed calls from Paige.

She checked the time and did a quick calculation…five p.m. London, two a.m. Sydney. Her spirits fell. What had Paige been up to? She hadn't left any messages, so there was no indication of what the trouble might be.

Setting her shopping bag and purse on the bed, Wendy removed her shoes—it was such a relief to get them off—and proceeded to call her daughter. There was no answer, so she left a message, letting Paige know it was okay to call back, and telling her that she was praying for her. Wendy knew that Paige wouldn't appreciate that, but she felt it important that Paige was aware she was in her mother's prayers.

If it wasn't the middle of the night in Sydney, she would have called Natalie. Instead, Wendy bowed her head and prayed for her youngest daughter. "Lord, I don't know what's happening with Paige right now, but You do. Please be with her, look after her, keep her safe. Let her make good decisions, but more than anything, dear Lord, I pray that she opens her heart to You and Your love. In Jesus' precious name. Amen."

When Wendy's eyes began to droop, she lay on her bed and closed them. It had already been a long and eventful day, and it wasn't over yet. She still had dinner with Bruce to look forward to. A power nap would do her good.

PAIGE'S PHONE rang just as Natalie arrived at the police station. She went to answer it, but the phone slipped out of her hand and landed on the tiled floor, shattering. She bent down to pick up the pieces, and when she straightened, Natalie was standing in front of her, disgust and disappointment on her face.

Natalie's eyes narrowed. "I don't appreciate being dragged out of bed in the middle of the night, Paige. I should have left you here."

"Why didn't you?"

"Because you're my sister and I promised Mum I'd look out for you, that's why."

"Mum just rang. I was trying to answer it..."

"Did you call her?" Natalie interrupted, sounding annoyed.

"Yes." Paige hiccupped.

"I told you not to bother her." Natalie's eyes narrowed further.

"I'm sorry. I forgot."

"Well, your phone's cactus. You won't be able to call her now," Natalie said.

"She'll be worried."

Natalie sighed heavily. "I'll call her in the morning. Let's get you out of here and into bed."

"Thank you." Paige hiccupped again.

Natalie helped her up. As they walked past the main counter, a wave of nausea rose from Paige's stomach. She couldn't hold it back and threw up all over the floor.

"I'm sorry," she said to both Natalie and the policeman who was staring at her like she was a piece of filth.

"Get 'er out o' 'ere," he yelled, waving his hand.

Natalie complied, and within minutes, Paige collapsed onto the back seat of Natalie's car and promptly fell asleep.

CHAPTER 10

*W*endy took more care than normal with her hair and make-up as she prepared for dinner with Bruce. Natalie had often encouraged her to wear some blusher and mascara as well as lipstick, but until now, she hadn't bothered. There'd been no need—Greg had always told her he loved her natural look. All of a sudden, she felt an urge to look attractive for Bruce. She rummaged in her cosmetic bag and found a wand of mascara. As expected, it was almost dry because of lack of use, but she managed to coax a small amount of the black goo onto her eyelashes. Then she brushed some of the light pink blusher that had never been used onto her cheeks and finished with a lick of lipstick. Stepping back from the mirror, she smiled at her reflection. Having a little more colour actually felt nice. She sprayed her hair lightly to keep it in place, and then dabbed some perfume on her wrists and the nape of her neck. She laughed at herself. It was almost like getting ready for a first date.

She'd chosen a dark skirt and a soft cream cashmere top, to which she almost added her set of pearls, but she quickly changed her mind. Greg had given the set to her for their twenty-fifth wedding anniversary. It wasn't appropriate to wear them. Instead, she clipped a brooch onto her top. Greg had given her that, too, but it held less sentiment than the pearls.

As she gazed at the brooch in the mirror, she thought of Greg. What would he think of Bruce? Would he approve? Would they have gotten on? She hoped so. They were both solid, kind, steadfast men, although different in so many ways. Greg had been a wonderful husband and provider, hard working and dedicated, but she sensed that life with Bruce would be full of adventure. She blinked. What was she thinking? Nothing could eventuate from this. It was a holiday romance, and when they parted at the end of the week, that would be it. Disappointment filled her. The truth was, she was falling in love, just like Bruce suggested, but how could it possibly work? She could never leave her children to live in Texas, and she doubted he'd leave his ranch to live in Sydney. They had no future together. Maybe she should end it right now. Not allow it to go any further. They'd both only end up hurt.

She glanced at her watch. If she was going, she needed to go —they'd agreed to meet in the foyer at seven p.m., so she'd be late if she didn't leave now. She let out a heavy sigh. If only she could learn to take a day at a time like Bruce said he did. And she'd prayed about this, asking God for wisdom and guidance. She needed to trust Him. Enjoy the moment, and leave the future in His hands. Her spirits lifted. That's what she'd do. She checked the mirror once more before grabbing her purse and coat and stepped out of her room into the corridor with a much lighter heart.

When the lift opened and she stepped into the foyer, Wendy quickly scanned the room for Bruce. Her heart warmed when she spied him. In his hat and boots, he looked so unlike anyone else, but that was one of the things that attracted her to him—he didn't care that he was different. He was his own man, confident in his own skin. He was chatting with a hotel staff member, and when his gaze caught hers, his face lit up and he beckoned her over.

"My, you're a sight for sore eyes." His eyes twinkled as he took her hand and drew her to his side. "I was just asking this fellow for some recommendations. He said we should eat at the Ox and Crown down the road. Isn't that right, Troy?"

"Yes, sir. They have a wonderful spread on Friday evenings, and there's also a live band."

"It sounds super. Thanks, son."

"You're more than welcome. Would you like me to call you a cab?" the young man asked.

Bruce deferred to Wendy.

"I'm happy to walk if it's not far," she said.

"And so am I, so no, we'll be fine, but thanks anyway." Bruce tipped his hat at Troy, and, slipping his arm around Wendy's shoulder, guided her towards the exit.

"You look lovely tonight, Wendy."

She felt her cheeks warm. Had he noticed her make-up, or was he just being polite? She smiled and thanked him, then tucked her hand into the crook of his elbow, leaning in close to squeeze through the crowd of people mingling on the footpath just outside the hotel. "I wonder what they're waiting for?" she asked.

"Troy said a group was going to a show tonight, so I guess they're waiting for the bus. Maybe we can go another night."

She smiled at him. "I'd like that."

They walked in silence until the crowd was far behind them. The fresh air cooled her face and she was glad she'd decided to wear her warm coat. They reached the hotel several minutes later, where Bruce requested a quiet table for two.

Wendy thought they might be turned away since the place seemed full, but she was relieved when the waitress showed them to a booth tucked in a corner towards the rear. She handed them menus and filled their glasses with water and said she'd return shortly to take their orders.

"This is nice," Wendy said, lifting her gaze.

He reached out and took her hand across the table, squeezing it. "It is. I couldn't wish for a more beautiful dinner companion." He winked at her, and she nervously chuckled before pulling her hand away and picking up her menu. "We'd better decide what we're having. She'll be back soon."

They perused the menus and made their choices. She opted for the fish of the day, and he chose the steak and chips. After placing their orders, Wendy remembered she hadn't told Bruce about Paige's phone calls. "I don't know what's going on with her, but it's so hard not to worry."

"You have a mother's caring heart, Wendy. I love that about you." The understanding in his voice brought a tear to her eye.

"Sometimes I think I care too much. I'm not sure I know how to let go," she said, trying to keep her voice steady.

"It's not easy. Not when they're flesh and blood and you want the best for them."

She drew a deep breath. He was so right. "Tell me about your boys." She knew he had three, but had only heard about the eldest, Nate, and a little about the youngest, Aiden. He'd mentioned the third, Andrew, very briefly.

He looked down, rapped his fingers on the table. What was holding him back? She reached out and took his hand. He looked up and met her gaze.

"You don't need to tell me if you don't want to," she said.

"I'm sorry. It's fine." He let out a sigh. "Andrew is Nate's twin. He was driving the day of my wife's accident, and he blames himself for his mother's death. He's never forgiven himself."

"That's so sad." Wendy's heart went out to the boy.

"It is. I've tried so hard to help him." Bruce paused, glanced away. "We all have, but we rarely see him these days, although he knows he's always welcome. He's carrying a load of anger and guilt, and all I can do is pray for him. He won't let anyone get close to him."

"Sounds a little like Paige, although she's not carrying guilt. I can't imagine how he must feel. I guess he still assumes that everyone blames him?" She angled her head. "Do they?"

Bruce wrapped his hands around his glass and stared at it. She shouldn't have asked…it was an intrusive question, but moments later, he looked up. "Honestly, it's been hard not to. He took a corner too fast and the truck rolled. We all told him over and over that he drove too fast, but he never listened. He was young and hot-headed. It was one thing to drive like that on his own, but completely irresponsible to drive recklessly with his mother beside him. They were on their way home from a shopping trip. Andrew offered to drive." Bruce's voice hitched, his eyes moistened.

Wendy squeezed his hand. "I'm so sorry for asking. It's not my business."

He drew a slow breath and seemed to settle. "It's okay, really. But yes, it took Nate and Aiden a long time to forgive Andrew. Especially when all he suffered from the wreck were some cuts and bruises, and Faith died instantly."

"How about you? How do you feel towards him?"

"I was in shock initially. Glad he survived, but angry he'd been driving too fast and caused Faith's death. I did blame him for a while. I did a lot of business with God over the following months. I knew I had to let go of that blame, but it wasn't easy."

"Has Andrew ever shown remorse?"

"Not really. He went on the defense at the time, blamed the curve of the road for the accident."

"Was he charged?" she asked.

"No. He wasn't speeding, just took the corner too fast. They said he wasn't at fault."

Their meals arrived, interrupting them. The waitress placed the plates on the table, and they smiled politely and thanked her.

Bruce straightened in his chair, pulling it closer to the table. "It was a horrid time, but you've gone through your own difficulty and sorrow, so you know what it's like."

"Yes, but Greg's death was different. We had no one to blame apart from God. And Paige still does."

"It's hard to let go, but don't give up hope for her." The look of understanding in Bruce's eyes brought tears to Wendy's. It was wonderful talking with someone who truly knew how she felt.

She smiled at him. "Nor you for Andrew."

"*Touché.*" He let out a deep sigh. "Let's pray, shall we?" He reached out and offered his hand.

Wendy nodded, placed her hand in his, and then bowed her head. Bruce took a few moments, she assumed to steady his thoughts and his heart, before he began. She knew his prayer of thanks would be even more heartfelt tonight following their discussion. When he started, his tone was quiet, reverent...

"Dear Heavenly Father, thank You for Your unending love, which none of us deserve. Thank You for our children whom we love so much, although it grieves us that some are far from You and yet are struggling with all that life has thrown at them. Lord, we give them to You, particularly my Andrew and Wendy's Paige, and ask that You'll draw them to Yourself, that You'll soften their hurting hearts." He paused, squeezed her hand gently. "And Lord God, I thank You for this wonderful woman You've brought into my life. Bless and guide us, dear Lord, and may we honor You in everything we do. And please bless this food to our bodies. In Jesus' precious name. Amen."

A tear welled in Wendy's eyes and her chest tightened. She took a moment to settle herself before looking up. Bruce was indeed a kindred spirit and she felt so blessed to have met him. When her gaze finally connected with his, a deep sense of peace flowed through her, and for now, she decided she'd treasure this special moment and let tomorrow take care of itself.

As they ate their meals, they continued chatting about their families. Aiden, Bruce's youngest son at twenty-seven years of age, was well adjusted and a regular church attender, although he'd suffered a severe crisis of faith following his mother's death. He was single, but had been in a long-term relationship with a girl until recently.

"He's a crop dusting pilot, and lives on the ranch, but in separate quarters," Bruce added.

"He sounds like a great young man."

"He is. And then there's Nate, whom I've told you a little about. He and his wife, Alyssa, have two young children."

"What do they call you?" she asked.

Bruce laughed. "They wanted to call me Pawpaw. I didn't fancy that, so now it's Papa."

"I like that. *Papa.*" A lump grew in Wendy's throat. Bruce's face shone with pride at speaking of them. He obviously loved his grandchildren. He'd never leave them... And if Natalie and Adam had children, how could she leave *her* grandchildren?

Trust Me...

Wendy sighed. Yes, very definitely, that's all she could do. She had to trust God to work this out, because she couldn't.

AFTER THEY FINISHED THEIR MEALS, Bruce held Wendy close while dancing slowly to the music the band was now playing. Her perfume tickled his nose while the feel of her body pressed against his sent his senses spinning. There was nothing about this woman he didn't love. He longed to hold her tight and kiss her passionately, but it was too soon. And besides, they weren't teenagers. Still, he couldn't deny the burning desire growing within him.

When they stepped outside the restaurant later that

evening, they both shivered. A cold wind had picked up. London weather was a far cry from what he was used to, but if it meant he could hold Wendy close, he didn't mind, so as they strolled back to the hotel, he wrapped his arm around her shoulders and held her tight.

Arriving at the hotel soon after, warmth enveloped them like a cozy blanket when they stepped through the doors. Bruce tipped his hat at the concierge and thanked him for the recommendation. Not wanting the night to end, he asked Wendy if she'd like to get a coffee.

She turned to him as they hovered in front of the elevator. "I'd love to, but I'm feeling quite weary. I think I need to go to bed. Do you mind?"

He smiled into her eyes, raised his hand and brushed her cheek lightly with his fingertips. "Of course not. It's been a lovely evening."

"It has. It's been wonderful. Thank you."

"Thank *you*." He lowered his face and pressed his lips gently against hers. They were soft and moist, and he so wanted to kiss her properly, but this wasn't the place. "Until tomorrow," he whispered.

"Until tomorrow." Her reply was barely audible.

THE FOLLOWING DAY, they shared breakfast together in the hotel's restaurant, a simple meal since no doubt there'd be a lavish spread at Elizabeth's party later in the day. Bruce had been slightly surprised when Wendy invited him to go with her, but he'd readily agreed. He wanted to go everywhere with her. Although he tried to take his own advice to take a day at a time, he couldn't help but think what would happen at the end of the week when she left to spend a few days in Paris, followed by another few in Florence and Venice, and he flew home to Texas. But it was hard to not think ahead. He'd never visited those cities before and would love to go with her. But would she agree?

They spent a leisurely morning on a boat tour down the Thames River. Wendy pointed out all the iconic landmarks to Bruce, and he enjoyed having her as his private tour guide. She knew so much about the history of all the places, but that wasn't surprising, since history was her specialty.

The morning passed, and then it was time for Elizabeth's party, which Wendy had told him was being held on the grounds of Elizabeth's home and hosted by her two daughters and their families. As the taxi cab pulled up under the portico of the stately manor, Bruce squeezed Wendy's hand. He knew she was anxious about reuniting with Greg's relatives, and reviving memories of him at every turn. He remembered what that had been like after Faith's passing. Even now, whenever he visited her elderly parents out at Willow Springs, and occasionally attended family get togethers, memories of all the wonderful times he and Faith had shared in the past flooded back and he had to face missing her all over again.

The taxi driver opened the door and Bruce climbed out. He thanked the driver and extended his hand to Wendy. He smiled at her as she scooted across the seat and stepped onto the gravel. She looked stunning in a pale blue chiffon pantsuit, and the string of pearls around her neck completed the outfit perfectly. He guessed they held a special place in her heart, but refrained from asking.

"Are you okay?" he asked as the taxi drove away.

"I think so." She returned his smile, but her mouth twitched slightly, and her hand was damp.

"I'm right beside you."

She squeezed his hand. "And I'm so grateful."

Bruce bent his arm and offered it to her. She slipped her hand into the crook of his elbow and held on tightly.

"I think I'm ready. Let's go," she said.

endy was so grateful that Bruce was with her at Elizabeth's party. Whilst it was wonderful catching up with relatives, it was also emotionally intense as each conveyed their sympathy over Greg's passing and asked how she was coping.

A few had raised their brows when she'd introduced Bruce as her friend from Texas she'd met in Dublin, but when he spoke easily with them, his charming southern manner won them over, and she was so pleased.

She and Bruce stole a quiet moment sometime during the afternoon and strolled around the gardens, which were beautifully manicured and a delight for the eyes. While they walked, hand-in-hand, Wendy's phone rang. She was tempted to ignore it but thought it might be Paige. "Do you mind?" she asked.

"Not at all," Bruce replied.

She quickly found the phone in her purse. Natalie's name

flashed on the screen, not Paige's. She swiped to take the call. "Natalie, how are you?"

"I'm fine, Mum. How are you?"

"Good. We're at Elizabeth's party."

"Oh, I'm sorry. I forgot... Did I hear you say *we?*" Natalie was speaking loudly, and she almost shouted the last word.

Wendy's eyes widened. She caught Bruce's amused gaze. She hadn't told any of her children that the man she'd met in Dublin had followed her to London. "Ah, yes..." How could she tell them now? But she couldn't lie. And besides, hadn't Natalie joked before she left about the possibility of Wendy meeting a handsome gentleman who'd sweep her off her feet? "Remember the man I told you about?"

"The one you met in Ireland?"

"Yes."

"And...?"

"He's here with me in London."

"Mum!"

"I know." Wendy could barely keep the mirth from her voice.

Natalie's voice lowered, almost to a whisper. "You're not doing anything silly, are you?"

"Natalie! Of course not."

"Well, I hope he's nice."

Wendy squeezed Bruce's hand as she smiled into his eyes. "He is. He's very nice. But what were you calling about, sweetheart?"

Natalie grew silent for a moment before she answered. "Paige got into trouble last night."

Wendy's heart fell and she immediately imagined the worst. "I knew it," she said quietly. "What did she do?"

"She got picked up for being drunk and disorderly in public."

Wendy sighed heavily. "She didn't hurt anybody, did she?"

"No, but she apparently smashed a window."

Wendy grimaced. "Oh dear."

"We bailed her out, and she has to face court in a week's time."

Wendy felt like a heavy weight was crushing her. "Should I come home?"

"No, please don't do that—we'll take care of her. Besides, you have your Texan cowboy to think of." Natalie's voice lifted, but Wendy groaned. Paige would never accept Bruce into their lives. Once again, Wendy internally chastised herself for living in a fantasy land. Maybe she really did need to end it right now, but when she caught Bruce's concerned gaze, she knew she couldn't. Paige would just need to face reality and grow up.

"Okay, I'll stay, but let me know if she gets worse. You know I'd drop everything to be there if I was needed."

"I do, but we'll cope, Mum. Enjoy your time away. I was angry that Paige tried to call you. I didn't want her bothering you."

"I'm glad I know what she did, even though it saddens me. I'll pray harder for her tonight."

"As will I. Love you, Mum. Take care."

"You too. Goodbye, love."

"Goodbye."

Wendy drew a deep, slow breath after ending the call. "Did you hear all of that?" she asked Bruce soberly.

"Enough."

"I feel so helpless."

He gently rubbed her arm. "I know how it feels."

"Do they ever learn?"

He smiled hopefully. "I'd like to think so."

"And did you hear what she said about you?"

He laughed. "I did. Texan cowboy!"

"Well, that's what you are."

"Yes, and you're my sweet Aussie gal." He swept her gently into his arms, and as their gazes met, her pulse throbbed double-time. She was powerless to resist when his lips brushed against hers. She returned his kiss with an eagerness that surprised her before pulling away. Breathless, she almost succumbed again as the tenderness in his eyes reached into the depths of her soul. "Bruce…"

"Shhh…it's okay. I'm sorry." His voice was soft, understanding. "I shouldn't have done that." He pulled her close and kissed the side of her head. "I've fallen in love with you, Wendy," he said quietly.

Resting her head against his chest, she took a moment to savour his words. Words she'd not expected to hear again. *Bruce loved her…* And if she was honest, she loved him, too, but she couldn't say it. Not yet, here in Greg's grandmother's home. It didn't seem quite right. Instead, she tightened her hold on him and sighed happily.

The rest of the afternoon passed with Wendy clinging to Bruce, drawing strength from their unexpected love. A lavish spread was laid out under a white gazebo, and as they ate and mingled, one of Elizabeth's great-grandsons played background music on her grand piano, which was positioned just inside the open French doors. It was a lovely party, and having Bruce by Wendy's side made it all the more enjoyable. He was the centre of attention for a while. Wendy guessed that not many of the guests had ever met a cowboy before, and he was plied with all types of questions which he readily answered.

While he was engrossed in conversation with one of Greg's male cousins, Wendy made her way over to Elizabeth. The guest of honour was seated in her favourite arm chair which had been brought outside for the occasion, and she was surrounded by a number of small children. She motioned for Wendy to draw up a chair beside her. The children made way for her and continued playing together on the floor.

"Your man seems popular." Elizabeth smiled as she extended her hand to Wendy.

Wendy laughed. *Her man...*It sounded surreal, but nice. "Yes, he's quite the attraction."

"You look happy, dear."

"Thank you, I *am* happy." *Apart from worry over Paige.*

"I'm so glad. I know I didn't remarry, but sometimes I wish I had. Being on your own can be lonely at times."

Wendy knew Elizabeth to be right on that account, because she'd experienced many lonely days and sleepless nights since Greg's passing, but talk of marriage sent her into a panic again. How could it possibly work? Natalie might accept Bruce, but what about Paige and Simon?

"Take your time, dear," Elizabeth counselled. "I can see the worry in your eyes. If you truly love each other, it will work out."

Wendy smiled appreciatively. "You still know me so well, even after the years apart."

"I do. It's a pity the rest of your family couldn't make it to England. I would have loved to see them again."

"You never know, maybe one day soon we can organise a family reunion." Somehow, Wendy doubted that would happen, but there was no harm in hoping.

"I'd like that." Elizabeth's voice faded and her eyes fluttered, eventually closing.

Wendy smiled, then gently withdrew her hand. Before she stepped away, she placed a light kiss on Elizabeth's forehead. "God bless you, dear lady."

She and Bruce took their leave soon after. As the taxi returned them to their hotel, she leaned against him, lost in thoughts and memories. Precious memories of times past she'd treasure forever, but Bruce was her future, of that she was growing more certain.

THEY SPENT the next few days visiting many of London's tourist spots—Buckingham Palace and the changing of the Guard, the London Eye, Houses of Parliament, the Tower of London, St. Paul's Cathedral, Westminster Abbey, and the British Museum and the National Gallery. They also ventured further afield to Oxford, Cambridge, and Bath. Wendy delighted in sharing the places she loved so much with Bruce and seeing the enjoyment on his face at each one. They ate at quaint cafés and cosy restaurants and fell deeper and deeper in love.

When he asked if he could go to Paris with her, she didn't hesitate. "Oh, yes, I'd love that."

He called his travel agent and changed his flights. Two days later, they arrived in Paris. They booked separate rooms in the Hotel Montparnasse and embarked on three wonderful days and nights in the city of love. Wendy pushed aside all thoughts of what would happen when their time together came to an end. She couldn't bear to think about parting ways, but with Paige constantly on her mind and in her prayers, she knew reality would come crashing down soon.

They climbed the Eiffel Tower, explored Sacré-Cœur and Montmartre, the hilly bohemian area abounding with narrow cobblestoned alleys, windmills, and artists. They joined a walking tour and learned about the history of the area, and had their portraits sketched by a young attractive woman who reminded Wendy a little of Paige. They spent a whole day at the Louvre, and then took an evening dinner cruise on the Seine. It was during the cruise that Bruce proposed, taking Wendy by complete and utter surprise.

They'd just finished their meal and were standing along the side of the boat, his arms wound around her waist from behind. He kissed her neck then slowly spun her around. Gazing into her eyes as the boat approached Pont Neuf, he drew a breath. "Wendy, you've captured my heart in a way I never expected. I love you so much, and I never want us to be apart. Will you marry me?"

Unable to speak, she searched his eyes. Moments passed. He was a gentle man, caring, kind and considerate, and she loved him. But could she marry him? The hope in his eyes turned to anguish. She had to respond. He was waiting. "Bruce, I...I don't know what to say. I love you, but..."

"I'm sorry, my sweet girl. I've jumped the gun again. Don't say anything. I've spoiled the moment."

"No, you haven't. But I need time to think. There are so many things to consider."

He lifted his hand and brushed her hair gently as he gazed into her eyes. "I understand. But we can work through whatever obstacles we might face."

"I like your confidence, and I wish I shared it."

"I've got enough for the two of us."

She laughed. "I think you have!"

He traced his finger over the curve of her face. "I love you, Wendy, but I won't pressure you. Give me an answer when you're ready."

"But we're running out of time."

"Yes, but we don't have to," he said.

"What do you mean?"

"Let me come to Venice with you."

She shook her head. It was hopeless. "It'll still be the same. I'll go back to Australia when the trip is over and you to the States. We'll still be apart at the end."

"Yes, but at least we'll have a few more days. And I've never been to Venice."

She laughed at the grin that spread across his face. "Is that all you want me for? To be your private tour guide?"

He stole a quick kiss. "I can't think of anyone I'd prefer more to be my guide."

She shook her head. "Well, since you're so full of compliments, I guess you're welcome to come along."

"Are you sure?"

She smiled. "Yes. Come to Venice with me."

CHAPTER 12

*V*enice was all that Bruce imagined it would be. Waterways and boats were everywhere, as well as the crowds, even though peak season was officially over. If it hadn't been for Wendy, he may not have bothered. He was starting to miss the wide open spaces of Texas, and was beginning to feel stifled with so many people in such a small area. Venice would almost fit into his ranch.

They stayed at a hotel just off the Grand Canal, within walking distance of Piazza San Marco. They strolled across countless bridges, explored the museums and places of interest, and caught *vaporettos*, the Venetian waterbuses, when their legs began to ache from so much walking and step climbing. They dined at fine restaurants with magic views of the city and surrounding area, and snacked at tiny, quaint cafés they came upon quite unexpectedly but drew them in with their enticing aroma of freshly brewed Italian coffee and pizza.

They avoided discussing the future, deciding simply to

enjoy each day together. On their last evening, however, on a gondola ride through the quieter canals, Bruce once again declared his love for Wendy. "I'll return to Texas, but my heart will go with you to Sydney." He nuzzled her neck as the gondolier guided the boat smoothly along a narrow canal, the slap of the oar on the water and the gondolier's quiet hum making Bruce more romantic than normal.

Wendy turned her head and looked at him, a sparkle in her eye. "You're such a smooth talker, Bruce McCarthy."

He laughed. "For a Texan, that's really sayin' somethin'." He tilted her chin, and leaning forward, kissed her slowly, treasuring every second of the magical moment. It wasn't a kiss of passion and urgency, but of one conveying his undying love. Her lips were soft and moist and her response gave him hope that one day she'd agree to be his wife.

WENDY STRUGGLED to retain composure as she and Bruce sat on the water bus taking them to Venice Marco Polo Airport early the following morning. This was it. Once her flight was called, they'd go their separate ways. They'd agreed to stay in contact via Skype and phone, but it wouldn't be the same. But she couldn't agree to marry him, not yet, at least. Not until she had time to pray about it more without the emotional pull of having him constantly with her, because maybe it *was* just a holiday romance. She wouldn't know, because she'd never had one, but she couldn't discount the possibility. She'd either miss him terribly and realise how much she loved him, and somehow, they'd work it out, or their love would fade, and that would be it. She prayed it would be the former, because the thought of never seeing him again ripped at her heart.

She clung to his hand and leaned in close, resting her head on his shoulder. She studied his hands, hardened and browned by years spent outdoors, and committed every sun spot, hair and wrinkle to memory.

The water bus pulled into the terminal and the passengers stood, and then waited for the walkways to be connected so they could disembark safely. Bruce offered Wendy his hand. She took it gladly, although there was no need. She'd soon be on her own, fending for herself as she returned to Australia. He placed his hand against the small of her back and guided her in front of him as they shuffled forward. How she wished they had more time. But she needed to go home. Although Paige had only received a large fine and a warning, Wendy felt she should be there for her. And Natalie's wedding was looming. And then there was Simon. He still hadn't said anything, but Wendy sensed that something truly was bothering him. Her family needed her more than she needed Bruce. Although her heart was telling her otherwise right now.

Finally, the walkway was in place and the passengers began quickly disembarking. No doubt some were in a hurry. She and Bruce had left themselves plenty of time, neither wanting the moment of separation to arrive, so they waited until the crush dissipated and followed behind slowly.

The airport was abuzz. Announcements blared from the overhead speakers every few minutes, and people scurried here and there, dragging overladen suitcases behind them. Babies cried, children laughed as they played around their parents' seats, but to Wendy, it was all just noise. She longed to sit quietly with Bruce, sharing their last moments together without the intrusion of anything else.

They had to check in at different counters. Parting for that short time was difficult enough—how would it be when they flew off in opposite directions? Bruce was waiting for her when she finished her check-in. Her heart warmed as her gaze took in the whole length of him, from his cowboy hat right down to his pointy boots. When their gazes connected and he smiled, her heart melted. He extended his hand, and she stepped forward and grasped it.

"My beautiful gal," he said.

She swallowed hard. "My handsome cowboy."

They found a quiet table tucked in the back of a busy café in the departures area and ordered coffee. An ache tore through Wendy's heart as she anticipated leaving him. They had ten minutes before her plane would be called. *Ten minutes.*

They sat opposite each other, his hand holding hers tightly across the table. Her heart pounded and she felt close to tears. They'd said all that needed to be said, and small talk didn't seem right. Instead, they sat quietly, communicating through their eyes and hands. Their coffees arrived and Bruce thanked the waitress, but the cups remained untouched on the table. Even drinking coffee seemed like small talk. He moved his seat next to hers and slipped his arm around her shoulders, pulling her tight. She rested her head on his shoulder. After several minutes of silent intimacy, her plane was called.

He walked with her to the boarding gate. Before she joined the line, he wrapped his arms around her and kissed her. "I love you, Wendy. I always will."

"And I love you." It was all she could say. She tore herself away and walked towards the gate attendant before she ended up in tears. She showed her boarding pass, turned and lifted her hand to her lips and blew a kiss to Bruce, then wiped her eyes as she walked down the walkway to the waiting plane.

Her flight was a long one...twenty-two hours plus, with a transit in Dubai. His, she knew, was much shorter at just four-teen hours. By the time she arrived in Sydney, Wendy was missing him so much she was tempted to call and tell him she'd marry him. But she knew her judgment was clouded by lack of sleep and her heightened emotional state. Time was needed to see things clearly, but if her heart had anything to do with it, she'd be marrying him before the year was over.

Natalie was waiting for her. Passing through the swinging doors was like returning from the magical world she'd lived in over the past three weeks and re-entering the real word. Much like how Peter, Susan, Edmund and Lucy must have felt when they returned from Narnia. Natalie hugged her and asked how she was.

"Tired." Wendy smiled at her daughter. "Thanks for meeting me."

"You're more than welcome. Now, let me help you." Natalie took Wendy's carry-on bag from her and hitched the strap over her shoulder. "So, tell me about your trip." She winked as they began pushing through the crowds.

Natalie obviously wanted to know about Bruce, but was Wendy ready to share her heart? Later, perhaps. Not now. She simply answered, "It was wonderful."

They reached Natalie's car, and after loading the luggage inside and buckling up, Natalie headed out of the multi-level car park Wendy had last been in with Paige three weeks before, and they joined the steady stream of cars heading into the city. The Sydney sky was clear and blue, a perfect spring morning, and as they crossed the harbour soon after, Wendy almost felt ready to be at home. Bruce had sent a text when he arrived at the ranch, and she'd sent him one after her plane landed. Even though she was with Natalie, she couldn't help but think what it would be like if Bruce was driving her home. Would he like Sydney? He was a country boy at heart, so maybe he wouldn't... She let out a heavy sigh. Much prayer was needed.

"How's Paige?" She'd last talked with her youngest daughter a week or so ago, but Paige had been less than forthcoming with any news. At least she'd been sober.

Natalie tapped the wheel with her index finger and stared straight ahead.

"What aren't you telling me?" Wendy asked, fixing her gaze on Natalie.

Natalie shot her a glance as she changed lanes. "You don't miss much, do you?"

"Not really. So...?"

Natalie let out a slow sigh. "She's dropped out of Uni."

Wendy's shoulders slumped. She'd been half-expecting that, but to hear it had actually happened was a real blow. At least when Paige was at Uni she was working towards a future and doing something, but now? "So, what's she doing instead?"

"Very little, I'm afraid. She's been hanging out with some Goths. Adam and I tried to talk sense to her, but she seems determined to rebel and do her own thing."

Wendy crossed her arms and turned to face the front. This

wasn't what she wanted to return to, but it was her life. *Goths!* Wendy didn't even know what they were.

"And Simon?" she eventually asked.

Natalie shrugged. "Uncommunicative as always."

"Thank goodness for you, Natalie." Wendy smiled at her daughter. "And how are *you?*"

"Good. Busy, but I'm fine. You don't need to worry about me."

"That's a relief. And the wedding preparations?"

"All in hand."

"Right." Wendy patted her stomach. "I need to lose some weight."

"Too much pizza?" Natalie grinned as she glanced at her mother.

Wendy chuckled. "You could say that."

"So, tell me about Bruce."

Wendy's heart fluttered at the very mention of his name. It had only been a day, but she was already missing him terribly. "What do you want to know?"

"What's he like?"

Wendy smiled as she pictured him in her mind. "Unique. He's a cowboy who loves the Lord. He loves his family, he misses his deceased wife. He's fun to be with."

"And from the sound of your voice, I believe you've fallen for him big time." Natalie reached over and squeezed her mother's hand. "I'm so happy for you, Mum. I think it's great." She smiled. "Invite him to the wedding. I'd love to meet him."

Wendy's heart skipped a beat. She hadn't considered that, but the thought excited her. "I don't know if I should. How would Paige react?"

"Don't worry about Paige. You have to do what's right for you. She'll come round eventually."

"I hope you're right."

Natalie turned onto Wendy's street and pulled into her driveway. "Home, sweet home." She smiled as she switched the car off. "I don't think Paige is home, if you're wondering."

"Right." Wendy refrained from asking where she might be this early in the morning. Better not to know right now. She opened her door and breathed in the salty harbour air. As she gazed down at the sparkling blue water, her thoughts immediately turned to the gondola ride with Bruce. It was a lifetime and a world away already. Stepping out of the car onto her driveway, she knew that the next few days would be filled with challenge as she readjusted to life at home. Life without Bruce.

CHAPTER 13

*B*ruce sat on his rocking chair on his veranda and gazed out at the wide open fields. Since being home, he'd found it hard to settle. Nate didn't need his help on the ranch, Aiden was off doing his own thing, although he dropped by often to have a chat, and he hadn't seen Andrew at all.

The two grandchildren seemed pleased to have him home and asked him to play games with them, which he happily did. His friends at church had greeted him warmly, and he soon returned to his normal routine of a weekly Bible study and church on Sundays, as well as the occasional committee meeting.

But his heart wasn't here. It was with Wendy, on the other side of the world. Each time her face appeared on his computer screen, he wanted to reach out and hold her. But he had to make do with simply looking at her and listening to her voice.

Nate hadn't paid much interest when Bruce told him about her, waving it off as if it was nothing, just an infatuation that would pass. "Nothing will come of it, Dad. You may as well forget about her." Alyssa, Bruce's daughter in-law, had shown more interest and asked him about Wendy. "She sounds nice. A pity she doesn't live closer." He couldn't agree more.

But Bruce knew that Wendy needed time. He'd assured her that he'd meant it when he asked her to marry him. He hadn't asked lightly, he truly loved her. They'd agreed to pray about it, separately and together, which they did. He felt right about it. He believed that their accidental meeting in Dublin that morning when he spilled coffee over her wasn't an accident, but a God ordained meeting. They were soul mates. She completed him. Made him a better man. He longed for the day when she felt the same. In the meantime, he prayed. And trusted. And remembered.

WENDY SLOWLY RETURNED to her life in Sydney. Paige continued to cause her great heartache with her lifestyle choices. She'd started dressing totally in black, dyed her hair even darker, and got piercings in places that made Wendy cringe. She slept during the day and went out at night. All Wendy could do was pray for her.

She'd seen Simon several times. He seemed almost normal, although he never invited her to his place—he always came to hers. She returned to her classes, but as she was lecturing on ancient Rome, she couldn't stop her thoughts from returning to those wonderful days and nights in Venice. *And Bruce.*

In church one Sunday morning, several weeks after returning, she closed her eyes and asked God what she should do. She'd been praying about whether or not to invite Bruce to Natalie and Adam's wedding, knowing it would be a huge turning point if she did. She needed to be sure it was what God wanted for them, and not just what she wanted.

The choir was singing one of her favourite hymns.

I come to the garden alone,
while the dew is still on the roses
And the voice I hear falling on my ear
The Son of God discloses.
And He walks with me, and He talks with me,
And He tells me I am His own;
And the joy we share as we tarry there,
None other has ever known.
He speaks, and the sound of His voice,
Is so sweet the birds hush their singing,
And the melody that He gave to me
Within my heart is ringing.

During the hymn, a sense of peace filled Wendy's spirit and she knew what she would do. She'd invite Bruce to the wedding. They were like-minded people who loved God and each other, and it seemed so right.

When she got home, she turned on her computer and called him. "How do you feel about coming to Natalie's wedding?"

His eyes widened. "Do you need ask?"

She laughed. "Not really. I take it that's a yes?"

"Yes, yes and yes!"

Wendy burst into tears and dabbed her eyes with a tissue.

"I'm sorry. I'm just so happy. It feels like we're meant to be together."

"I know, my darling. I've been praying for this moment for weeks. I'll book my ticket tomorrow."

WENDY TELEPHONED Natalie and told her.

"I'm so glad, Mum. You've been like a bear with a sore head since you've come home."

"I have not."

"You haven't been terribly happy."

Wendy smiled at her daughter's perception. "You're right, love. I haven't been. I'm sorry."

"You're in love, Mum. It's okay."

"That sounds so strange, but yes, I've missed him so much."

"Well, I for one am looking forward to meeting your cowboy."

Wendy chuckled, but then sobered. "Paige won't be, that's for sure."

"Don't worry about her," Natalie said.

"But I do, you know that."

"Yes, I know, and so do I, but she's not going to change until she's ready."

Wendy let out a sigh. Natalie was right, but it grieved her so much to see Paige self-destructing. She didn't know her daughter anymore, but despite not liking Paige's chosen life-style, Wendy loved her and wanted her to find true happiness. She knew that underneath Paige's hard exterior was a little girl who was hurting terribly.

. . .

THE NEXT FEW weeks passed in a flurry of preparation. Wendy rejoined the gym and started an exercise regime. She also began eating better, determined to lose the weight she'd stacked on while overseas. She wanted to look her best for Bruce.

The day finally came. She could barely breathe as she waited at the airport for his plane to land. Natalie had wanted to come with her, but Wendy said she'd prefer to meet him on her own. "You'll meet him soon enough."

"It's okay, Mum. It's funny seeing you acting like a teenager in love."

"I am not."

Natalie laughed. "Yes, you are! But it's all good. I'm so excited for you."

Wendy chuckled at recalling their conversation. Before she could grow nervous again, the screen showing arrivals flashed that his plane had landed. With her heart beating out a staccato, she waited for a text. It came soon enough.

Just landed...see you soon. Love you xx.

She quickly replied. *Can't wait to see you. Love you too xx*

She was breathless as she scanned the passengers streaming through the doors. And then she saw him. She waved and ran towards him. He dropped his bags and encircled her with his arms, hugging her and kissing her cheek. She returned his hug and then wiped her misty eyes. "Welcome to Australia," she said. "It's wonderful to see you."

"And you're a sight for sore eyes." He pulled her close again and kissed the top of her head. "Come on, let's get out of here."

They walked out of the terminal together, arm in arm. Wendy kept snatching glances of him to make sure he was really there. Touching him each time was so surreal. Each time their gazes connected, the smiles they shared warmed her heart.

She'd arranged for him to stay in the motel not far from her house. It had been so tempting to have him stay with her, but it wouldn't have been proper. They had to do things God's way, even if it was hard. How could they ask Him to bless their relationship if they didn't do what was acceptable in His eyes? But that didn't mean he couldn't visit, and after checking him into the motel, she drove them the short distance to her home. She'd invited Natalie and Adam for dinner, but had prepared a light lunch just for the two of them.

When she pulled into her driveway, Rose, her elderly neighbour, was outside and waved. Wendy laughed when Rose's eyes widened as Bruce tipped his cowboy hat to her. "The tongues will start wagging now," she said. "Rose is quite the neighbourhood busybody."

"I'd better go introduce myself then."

"Time enough for that later." She stopped the car in the garage and turned the engine off. The electricity between them was real and tangible. She wanted to lean into him and give him a deep passionate kiss, but she pushed the door open and climbed out instead. "Come inside and freshen up."

"Do I smell that bad?" He tilted his head.

"I didn't mean that..." When he winked, she knew he was teasing, and laughed.

As WENDY CLIMBED out of the car, she noticed Simon's boxes were still stacked against the wall. Muffin meowed when she opened the house door. As Bruce followed her inside, she wondered what he thought. This was the home she'd shared with Greg. Raised their children in. Family photos hung on the walls, and he was in them. She guessed that photos of Bruce's wife still hung on the walls of his home, too. Probably always would. How could you forget your first love? It was impossible, but like Elizabeth said, it didn't mean you could never love another.

She set her handbag down on the kitchen counter and turned the kettle on while Bruce gazed around.

"This is one lovely home, Wendy."

She smiled. "Thank you. I love it, but it's quite big now the children have all gone." Paige had moved out just a week earlier and moved in with her new boyfriend, a Goth she hadn't brought home to meet her mum. Although it tore at Wendy's heart, she had to let her go. Trying to force her to stay wouldn't achieve anything except bad feelings.

"Never considered selling?" He removed his hat and wandered through the living room, stopping in front of the glass doors leading out to the deck.

She had to wonder at the question. Did he really mean, would she sell it and move to Texas? If so, she still wasn't sure. She answered simply, "Not really, but I might one day."

He turned around and walked back to her. Slipped his arms around her waist, gazed into her eyes. "I've been waiting for this moment for over a month." He lowered his mouth and kissed her gently.

CHAPTER 14

*B*ruce loved everything about Sydney. It helped that Wendy lived there, but he didn't even mind that it was a city. She'd told him it didn't take long to reach the country areas if he ever needed to get out of the hustle and bustle for a while. The weekend after he arrived, he took her up on the suggestion and they drove to the Blue Mountains, several hours west. They stayed in a guest house, in separate rooms, and spent a wonderful weekend together exploring the area renowned for its beautiful scenery, majestic mountains, and quaint cafés. They even did some hiking.

Bruce grew more convinced that he and Wendy should spend the rest of their lives together as husband and wife, but he didn't pressure her. He trusted that she'd come to the same conclusion eventually, and in the meantime, he vowed to be patient.

Her daughter, Natalie, and Natalie's fiancé, Adam, had welcomed him with open arms, just as Wendy had told him they would. He'd briefly met Simon, who'd looked him over suspiciously, but seemed to warm to him a little when he heard about the ranch and all the cattle they ran. Paige had refused to meet him. It was to be expected. Losing a parent was hard, and welcoming the potential new partner of your remaining parent wasn't easy, especially if there were still underlying issues that hadn't been dealt with. She was a challenge, for both of them.

During the week leading up to the wedding, Wendy had warned him she'd be busy. He told her he didn't mind, he'd be happy on his own and didn't need molly coddlin' all the time. She laughed, and then leaned in for a hug. How he loved her.

On the Wednesday of that week, he received news from home that Aiden's plane had crashed. He was okay, but was in the hospital with a broken leg and multiple cuts and bruises. He was fortunate to be alive. Bruce was torn. Should he go home to be with his son? Nate told him in no uncertain words that was where he should be. He'd been less than happy when Bruce told him he was flying to Australia, anyway. But Bruce couldn't leave Wendy. Not now, with the wedding in just a few days' time. Instead, he called Aiden in the hospital and spoke to him.

"Son, are you okay?"

"Yes, and I'm thankful to be alive."

"What happened?"

"The plane stalled and then dived. I controlled it enough and landed, but not on a field. I crashed into a barn."

"Well, the good Lord was lookin' out for you, that's all I can say."

"He was indeed."

"Do you need me to come home? Nate said I should."

Aiden groaned. "He would. No, don't spoil your trip. I'm okay. Besides, I don't think your lady friend would be too happy if you left so soon. How's it goin'?"

Bruce smiled. Aiden was the only one who'd supported him when he broke the news he was going to Sydney. "It's goin' good."

"Proposed yet?"

Bruce chuckled. "I did that a long time ago."

"And she hasn't said yes?"

"Not yet."

"Maybe soon?"

"Maybe," Bruce replied hopefully.

"I'll be prayin' for you."

"And me for you. Take care, son. God bless."

"God bless you, too, Dad. Love you."

"Love you too, son." Bruce ended the call and bowed his head in prayer. "Dear Lord, take care of my son, Aiden. He's a good man, and he loves You. Heal his body and please forgive me for not goin' home to be with him. And Lord, I pray for Nate and Alyssa and am thankful that they love You, too. Bless them and the children, and last but not least, I pray for Andrew. Help him to forgive himself and to find peace and purpose in his life. I know that only You can truly give him that, so Lord, I ask that his heart will be open to Your love.

"And I pray for Wendy. Thank You for bringing her into my life. Bless her and her family. She loves them all so much, but they also cause her great concern at times. Please let her find rest in You, dear Lord, and help her to entrust her children to You. And please give her peace about our relationship, as You've given me peace. You know how much I love her and want to marry her. Please help us work it out. In Jesus' precious name. Amen."

~

THE DAY of Natalie and Adam's wedding finally came. Wendy rose early, showered and dressed in the clothes she'd set out the night before, made a quick cup of tea to drink while she had a short quiet time and prayed blessings over Natalie and Adam on their special day, and then headed out to pick up Bruce. They'd agreed to have breakfast together at Wendy's favourite café in a secluded cove on the harbour before she headed off to spend the morning with Natalie, Paige, *if she decided to turn up*, and Natalie's other bridesmaid, Sandra, Natalie's closest friend.

Bruce was waiting outside the motel when Wendy arrived, and her heart fluttered as it always did whenever she saw him. To have him here, in her home town, was surreal, but wonderful. She stopped the car and he climbed in, leaning over to kiss her on the lips. "Good morning, darling." His gentle voice and tender smile caused her stomach to flip and she couldn't help but think how nice it would be to wake up beside him each morning.

She drew a slow breath and settled herself. "And good morning to you, my love."

He fastened his seatbelt and she drove off. The café was nearby, so within a couple of minutes they were settling into a table on the alfresco deck overlooking the glistening water. A light breeze came off the water, and the jangle from the halyards on the yachts moored in the protected waters sounded peaceful and inviting. The day was perfect. Endless blue skies with just some light wispy clouds on the horizon.

Wendy sighed with happiness as she shifted her gaze to Bruce. She knew he was waiting for an answer to his proposal, but he hadn't placed her under any pressure, and she appreciated that. The thought of all the complications that would arise if they married caused her some anxiety, but she also knew that if they married, they would face them together, and that comforted her. Bruce was a gentle man, but of strong character. So, what was she waiting for? Wendy sighed again. She wasn't really sure.

They ordered breakfast—Wendy chose salmon and avocado on light rye sourdough, and Bruce selected the Big Breakfast—sausages, bacon, eggs, mushrooms and tomatoes on two pieces of thick toast. Wendy laughed. His appetite was as hearty as Greg's had been.

While they waited, Bruce took her hand and stroked it gently. She loved the feel and strength of his hand. He'd told her that cancer and the treatments had knocked him around physically, but Wendy couldn't see it. To her, he was strong and handsome. She smiled. "I'm so glad you came."

"And I'm so glad you asked me."

Time stood still. Her heart thumped. It was such a perfect, romantic setting. They were alone, other than a woman drinking coffee at the other end of the deck. She cleared her throat, but then their breakfasts arrived. Wendy released the breath she'd been holding. She'd come so close to telling Bruce she would accept his proposal.

He gave thanks as he always did before they ate. She loved hearing him pray. He spoke from the heart, sincere and humble. His simple but unswerving faith encouraged her greatly in her own relationship with God.

They chatted about the day as they ate their breakfast and sipped on coffee. Robyn, Wendy's friend, had offered to look after Bruce for the morning and then drive him to the wedding. Not that he needed looking after, but Wendy thought it would be nice for them get to know each other. Robyn had been on her own for years since her divorce and was always good company.

When Wendy dropped him at Robyn's place a short while later, her hand lingered in his and unspoken words passed between them. They'd hardly been apart since he arrived in Australia. The end of the school term had coincided nicely with his arrival, meaning she didn't need to go to work.

"Take care of him, Rob," Wendy said, tearing her gaze from his to smile at her friend.

"I'll be sure to. I've got a few fun things planned."

"Oh yes?" Wendy laughed, her forehead creasing. "Like what?"

"Oh, maybe a round or two of golf, followed by a nice lunch."

"Sounds great. Enjoy." Wendy squeezed Bruce's hand and met his gaze. "And I'll see *you* at the church."

"I'll look forward to it." He returned her squeeze and smiled into her eyes, causing her heart to once more pick up its pace.

As she drove away and headed to Natalie's apartment, she prayed once more for guidance, knowing she needed to give him an answer very soon.

When Natalie opened the door, Wendy's heart fell. Instead of a happy, smiling bride-to-be, Natalie's eyes were red and puffy. Wendy stepped forward and wrapped her arms around her daughter. "What's wrong, sweetheart?"

"Oh, Mum. Everything's gone wrong. The florist called and said she couldn't get the orchids I wanted for the bridemaids' bouquets, the hairdresser's running late, and Paige hasn't turned up, and...and I think I've got cold feet." She began sobbing into Wendy's shoulder.

Wendy pulled her tight and rubbed her back. "There, there, my darling. Let it out. It's okay." She spoke soothingly to calm her distraught daughter. "It's just wedding nerves, that's all. We've all had them."

Natalie's sobs eased a little. She dabbed her eyes and straightened. "But everything was so organised. I don't understand how it's all gone amuck now."

"Sometimes it doesn't matter how well organised you are, things happen that are out of our control. You know that."

Natalie nodded. "But I so wanted today to be perfect."

"And it will be. Trust me." Wendy placed her arm around Natalie's shoulder. "Let's go inside and I'll make a cup of tea. Is Sandy here?"

"She's on her way."

Wendy frowned. "So, you've been here on your own?"

"Yes. She had to go home last night because Harry's teething and Jacob couldn't settle him." Jacob was Sandy's husband and Harry, their son.

"And no Paige?"

"No Paige. I doubt she'll come."

Wendy sent up a silent prayer for her youngest daughter. In many ways, it would be less stressful if she didn't come, but she needed to be there—it was her sister's wedding, after all. "You should have called me. I would have stayed with you." Wendy stepped into the kitchen and turned the kettle on.

"I didn't want to interfere with your time with Bruce."

"He would have understood. And it's not like he was staying over."

"Maybe I should have called."

"Well, it's too late now. But what's this about getting cold feet? Sit down and tell me what's troubling you."

Natalie pulled out a stool and gratefully accepted the tea Wendy set in front of her. Wendy pulled up a stool and sat beside her.

"Oh, I don't know...I'm just not sure I'm doing the right thing."

"But you love Adam, I know you do, and he loves you. You're so good together."

"Maybe that's the problem. We've never had an argument, but we've never been like you and Bruce, either."

Wendy frowned. "What do you mean?"

"You're always hugging and kissing and you seem so much in love. Adam and I aren't like that."

Wendy chuckled. "And neither were your dad and I. We were much more reserved. I don't know why it's different with Bruce. You'd think at our age we wouldn't be showing so much affection in public."

"You're in love, Mum." Natalie smiled, looked a little brighter. She leaned forward. "So, are you going to marry him?"

Wendy inhaled slowly. It was the question that had been tormenting her since that night in Paris. She'd told Natalie one night when they were out shopping and having coffee that

Bruce had popped the question. "I don't know, sweetheart. We've avoided talking about it, but I know he's waiting for an answer."

"Have you talked about where you'd live?"

"Not really. He just said we'd work it out."

"Maybe you should discuss it."

"Maybe you're right. I can't bear the thought of leaving you all and living half-way around the world. And I can't see him leaving his ranch."

"You might be surprised."

Wendy nodded. "Maybe."

A soft knock on the door interrupted them. Wendy grabbed Natalie's hand as Natalie stood to answer it. "It will be fine, sweetheart. You and Adam are going to have a long, happy marriage. And you can always spice things up a bit by showing more affection." Wendy winked at her.

Natalie's cheeks turned pink. "Mum!"

Wendy laughed. "A good dose of romance never hurt anyone. It makes you feel good."

"Okay…I'll remember that." Natalie grinned as she headed for the door. "Sandy! Come in."

And so it began. The morning passed with lots of laughs, coffee, and croissants. Hair was done, faces made up. The flowers arrived and Natalie loved them, despite the brides-maids' bouquets missing the orchids. And Paige arrived. Not in time to have her hair or make-up done, but in time to put on her dress which she said countless times looked terrible on her. Both Wendy and Natalie gave up telling her she looked beautiful. Her black hair shone, and even though she left the piercings in her ears, she removed the ring from her nose and agreed to put on some pink lipstick instead of the black she normally wore.

Wendy gave her a hug and told her she loved her. Paige prickled a little but seemed happy in her own way that she wasn't being judged.

And then it was time for Natalie to put on her wedding gown. The gown fit her perfectly and she looked absolutely gorgeous. Roxanne, the designer, had done a wonderful job.

Simon arrived on time. Wendy was pleased that Natalie had set aside her grievances with him and asked him to walk her down the aisle.

"I wish Dad was here to walk with me," she'd said to Wendy a little earlier when they shared a quiet moment together.

Wendy rubbed her arm. "We all do, sweetheart, believe me. But he's here with us in spirit. He would have been so proud of you." Wendy blinked back tears, as did Natalie.

The photographer arrived and took copious shots. Wendy was relieved that her dress fit. The hours at the gym had paid off, and she felt very feminine in the soft, flowing, light blue dress Roxanne had made for her, and she hoped Bruce would like it.

Soon it was time to leave. The cars were waiting outside. Wendy, Paige and Sandy went in one, Natalie and Simon in the other. Before Natalie stepped into the car, Wendy gave her a big hug. "You look stunning, sweetheart. Your dad would be so proud, and Adam won't be able to keep his hands off you tonight."

Natalie blushed and then laughed. "Thanks, Mum. That's made my day." She then carefully climbed into the back of the car, followed by Simon.

In the other car, Wendy squeezed Paige's hand and held it. She gave her a smile and prayed silently for her daughter. It still concerned her how Paige would cope if she decided to marry Bruce, but she was beginning to think that if Bruce could win Paige over with his charm, it might help her let go of the anger over losing her dad. It was a long shot, but anything was possible with God. It was definitely worth asking Him about.

They arrived at the church, the church Wendy and Greg had married in, the one that their children had been raised in, the one that she, Natalie, and Adam still attended. Like she'd done in London, Wendy knew she needed to keep her memories and sentiment under control. Today was her daughter's special day, a time of commitment and celebration and looking to the future, not one of regret or sadness. She squeezed Paige's hand again and stepped out of the car.

CHAPTER 15

*W*endy looked stunning. Bruce couldn't take his eyes off her as she entered the chapel. Her eyes sparkled as she greeted guests on either side of the aisle and paused to chat briefly with each. When their gazes met, he smiled and her face lit up, filling his heart with warmth. Finally reaching his pew, she sat beside him. He took her hand and squeezed it. "You look lovely, my darling."

"Thank you. And you clean up very well yourself." She gave him a wink.

He'd brought his one and only suit for this moment, and even though he was a jeans and boots man, he was glad he'd dressed suitably. Wendy linked her arm through his, he took her hand. He sensed she was almost ready to give him an answer. Natalie's impending wedding would have made her think more about her own situation. He prayed that soon she would be walking down the aisle toward him, and he'd be standing where Adam now stood, anxiously awaiting his bride.

The organist changed tunes and everyone stood. Bruce turned his head and placed his hand lightly on Wendy's hip as she leaned against him. He'd almost expected her to not show any physical affection while they were around friends and family, but she seemed proud of him, and that made him glad. And hopeful.

Bruce blinked when the first bridesmaid entered. "Is that Paige?" he whispered into Wendy's ear.

Wendy nodded. He felt her body visibly relax as Paige walked slowly down the aisle. She'd been so concerned that Paige wouldn't turn up for the wedding, but here she was, stunningly beautiful with long, jet black hair and a smile he would never have expected, based on how Wendy had described her demeanor. Perhaps she was putting on an act, doing the right thing, but whatever it was, she was here, and Wendy was obviously relieved, and that made him happy.

Paige turned her head slightly when she approached the front and caught her mother's gaze. It shifted to him and her smile faltered. There'd be a lot of work to do to win her over—but he'd leave it with the Lord to soften her heart...*in His time.* He wouldn't force a relationship.

The other bridesmaid followed, and then Natalie appeared in the entrance on Simon's arm. Her father should have been here, but he wasn't. Bruce knew how hard an occasion like this was when a loved one was missing. Faith wasn't there when Nate married Alyssa, and it was heart wrenching. He hadn't expected Andrew to attend, just like Wendy had had doubts about Paige, but at the last moment, he'd arrived. They'd all been glad, but Andrew left half-way through the reception. Bruce assumed because there was no alcohol. Yes, it was hard, and nothing would change the hole that an absent parent left in their hearts. He prayed silently for Wendy's family, that they would each know the peace that passeth all understanding... the peace that only God could give.

Natalie, poised and beautiful in her stunning gown, smiled at her mother as she passed. Wendy dabbed her eyes. Bruce rubbed her arm.

After Natalie reached Adam, Simon kissed her cheek and then left her to slide into the pew next to his mother. Wendy slipped her arm around his waist. Her love for her children was so evident, and Bruce knew that leaving them behind was a huge reason for hesitating to marry him. But having spent the last couple of weeks in Sydney, he was starting to think he could live here. He'd miss the ranch and his family, for sure, but they could visit at least once a year. And maybe she'd agree to return to the ranch during her breaks from school, where they could enjoy extended vacations. They'd work it out, of that he was sure. If only she'd say yes...

WENDY STRUGGLED to contain her emotions as Pastor Will McDougall began the ceremony. Natalie and Adam stood before him, holding hands, while she sat in the pew holding Bruce's. She couldn't stop herself from thinking that everything Pastor Will said could apply to her and Bruce. "Two lives, two hearts, joined together in friendship, united forever in love. There is only one happiness in life, to love and be loved. God is love, and whoever dwells in love dwells in God.

"Dearly beloved, we're gathered here today in the sight of

God and man to join this man and this woman in holy matrimony. Not to be entered into lightly, holy matrimony should be entered into with solemn reverence and honour. Marriage is a sacred union between husband and wife. It's the basis of a stable and loving relationship, and is the joining of two hearts, bodies and souls. The husband and wife should support one another and provide love and care for each other in times of joy and in times of adversity..."

Wendy dabbed her eyes when Adam vowed to love and cherish Natalie for the rest of his life. She prayed that he'd also give her daughter the romance she craved. That he'd loosen up a little and not be quite so serious. Just like the man sitting beside her. Wendy leaned closer to him. Her heart pounded as Natalie said her vows, and in that moment, Wendy knew with deep certainty that she would marry Bruce.

Later, at the reception at the Buena Vista Gardens perched on a cliff high above the stunning harbour, Wendy drew Bruce aside and linked her arm through his. "Walk with me?"

"Sure..." He gave her a puzzled look but strolled happily beside her as she led him to a secluded alcove. The smell of jasmine wafted in the air, carried by a soft breeze. It was the perfect setting to give him the answer he was waiting for. She faced him, held his hands in hers, met his gaze. Her heart thudded, but she knew beyond a doubt that she loved him heart and soul. God had brought them together that day in Dublin, a chance meeting that had changed their lives forever.

She swallowed hard. "I've thought long and hard about this, my darling, and I'm sorry I've taken so long to reply to your proposal." She swallowed again. "The answer to your question is yes, I'll marry you. You're my soul mate, and I love you with my whole being, and I want to be your wife."

His eyes moistened. He lifted his hands and cupped her face. Gazed deeply into her eyes. "My beautiful girl. I love you so much, and I can't wait to be your husband. I'll look after you always, for as long as I live. And I'll treasure this moment forever." He lowered his mouth and pressed his lips gently against hers. His kiss was slow and held so much love. She didn't want the moment to end, but it was only a beginning. They had the rest of their lives to spend together, and Wendy knew it would be full of romance and love. Her Texan cowboy might have a tough exterior, but he was a romantic at heart, and the prospect of spending a lifetime with him thrilled her.

CHAPTER 16

*H*aving made the decision to spend the rest of their lives together, Wendy and Bruce wasted no time planning their wedding. Wanting somewhere neutral where both families would feel comfortable and have the chance to get to know each other in a relaxed setting, they decided on a Fijian wedding.

Wendy engaged Roxanne to design her outfit. She suggested a simple but elegant pantsuit in a soft floral chiffon. Wendy was delighted with the result, although she'd been a little concerned Roxanne might not deliver on time. There was no need to worry, however. She had it ready with two weeks to spare.

Bruce had reluctantly returned home to Texas several weeks after Natalie and Adam's wedding. Neither he nor Wendy had wanted to part, but they both knew he needed to spend time with his family before moving to Sydney, especially when only Aiden and Alyssa had encouraged him to accept

Wendy's invitation to her daughter's wedding. "I'll have some convincin' to do, that's for sure," he'd said on their last evening together before he flew home. "But as soon as they meet you, they'll know why I love you so much."

Wendy had laughed at that, especially when he stole a kiss from her. "Oh, you're a smooth talker, Bruce McCarthy."

He stuck his lip out. "But I mean it."

She laughed again, and then grew serious. "I'm going to miss you."

"Not as much as I'm going to miss you."

Their gazes locked, and for a moment, time stood still. How had this man come into her life and swept her off her feet? To have had one wonderful husband was more than many women could ever hope for, but she was indeed blessed to now have the opportunity to spend the rest of her life with another amazing man.

He pulled her close and kissed the top of her head. She cherished the moment, because that might be all they had. She knew there was risk in marrying him. He'd assured her that he was completely clear of cancer, but she knew there was every possibility it could return. There was no guarantee of tomorrow for either of them, so every moment of every day was precious.

At the airport the following day, he'd gazed into her eyes and smiled. "Until Fiji."

She returned his smile, fighting tears. "Until Fiji."

And now, here they were. Wendy and her family had arrived earlier that morning, and she was eagerly waiting for his plane to land. Natalie had come with her to the airport, just a twenty-minute drive from the resort on the island of Viti Levu. Adam, Simon and Paige had stayed behind.

Wendy could hardly contain her excitement as the plane taxied towards the terminal. She kept pinching herself that this was really happening. That Bruce and his family were about to disembark, and that tomorrow, she'd be marrying her Texan cowboy, as her family now called him. But her excitement was tinged with a little worry. *Would his family like her?* Bruce had assured her over and over again that they'd love her, but she was less than certain. She knew how her family would feel if she told them she was marrying an American and moving to Texas. She could only guess that his felt at least some resentment towards her.

She'd prayed about it continually, because the last thing she wanted to do was drive a wedge between Bruce and his family. It was something they needed God to work out. Just like everything, really. Wendy had been learning that letting go and trusting God was much better than trying to work everything out herself. Even with Paige, she'd seen a change since she stepped back a little. For the first time ever, Paige had ended a relationship and had now been single for almost a month. Not long, but a record for her. And she hadn't dyed her hair for almost three weeks. Wendy smiled as she thanked God for these changes. Small as they might be, they gave hope that Paige might have started on the path to healing and wholeness.

But then there was Simon. She let out a heavy sigh. He'd been ambivalent when she and Bruce announced their engagement, and then reluctant to attend the wedding. It was only Adam's intervention that had gotten him here. *How could he have not wanted to come to Fiji?* It was such a beautiful place, and it was such a special occasion. At least, she and Bruce thought so! But he'd come, unlike Andrew. Bruce had said it was probably for the best, but Wendy knew he was disappointed. Still, Nate, Alyssa, their two children, and Aiden, were coming. And now they were here! Wendy waved excitedly as Bruce emerged from the walkway. His face lit up with the smile she'd come to love. He removed his hat and wrapped his arms around her. Held her tight. Kissed her.

Such happiness filled her heart as she gazed into his eyes. "It's so wonderful to see you," she said.

He introduced her to his family. Nate, Alyssa, the two children, Liza and Larry, and Aiden. They all hugged her and smiled. Nate and Aiden looked so much like Bruce she was slightly taken aback. It was mainly the eyes. Crystal blue with a sparkle, although Nate's sparkle seemed slightly dim as he jiggled Liza on his hip. Wendy sensed that Nate was the one she needed to win over the most. Alyssa seemed sweet, and after hugging Wendy, she immediately began chatting with Natalie.

The group headed outside. Wendy sighed contentedly as Bruce slipped his arm around her shoulder and pulled her close to his side.

WENDY AND NATALIE had driven to the airport, but the resort provided a free shuttle, so Natalie joined Bruce's family in the shuttle, allowing Bruce to drive back with Wendy. Alone in the car, he pulled her close and brushed a gentle kiss across her lips. She closed her eyes, anticipating their future. She sighed happily. "Come on, we can't sit here all day."

"I don't know why not," he whispered, his breath warm on her cheek.

She chuckled. "Because we're in an airport carpark, that's why!"

He laughed. "Okay. Show me the way." Straightening, he started the engine and headed out of the carpark onto the road.

"Don't forget to stay on the left," she reminded him.

"Roger that," he replied with a wink.

They drove the short distance to the resort, and soon, Bruce and his family had checked in and were settling in around the pool for some down time. The children swam and splashed and had so much fun. The adults engaged in conversation while sipping on iced teas and tropical juices. Some of the conversation was a little stilted, but nevertheless, they were together, getting to know each other and, Wendy prayed, accepting her and Bruce as a couple.

The afternoon and evening passed, and when it was almost time to retire, Bruce asked if she'd take a stroll along the beach with him.

"I'd love to," she replied.

The moon was out and shone on the water that gently lapped on the beach. It was just like she'd always imagined a Fijian beach to be like, warm and sultry, and oh, so romantic. She leaned into Bruce as sand squelched between her toes.

They stopped halfway along and he pulled her close. Gazed into her eyes. "Wendy, are you sure about this? You have no doubts?"

She kept her gaze steady. Natalie and Robyn had asked her the same question many times over, and each time, she'd told them she was one-hundred percent sure. She smiled at him. "No doubts. I love you with all my heart."

He smiled back. "And I you. I can't wait until we're married, but I can barely believe it's happening."

"I know. It's surreal. Especially being here."

"I can't think of anywhere I'd rather be right now."

She laughed lightly. "Neither can I."

His lips met hers in a soft, tender kiss. "Until tomorrow."

"Until tomorrow."

THE FOLLOWING DAY, Wendy and her family joined Bruce and his family for a pre-wedding breakfast at the resort's alfresco dining room positioned alongside the beach. She was pleased at how everyone was getting along, especially Paige and Aiden. In fact, watching them made her smile. Maybe God had something planned for them.

They'd planned a mid-morning wedding on the beach, so once breakfast was over, they went their separate ways to prepare for the occasion. Natalie and Paige helped Wendy, not that there was much to do. She allowed Paige to apply some light make-up, and Natalie did her hair, placing a sweet-smelling frangipani flower behind her ear.

And then it was time. Wendy had asked Simon to walk with her across the sand, and as they waited under the shade of palm trees, she turned to him. "Simon, I know you're not completely happy, but please know that just because I'm getting married, nothing will change between us. I'll always be here for you, no matter what. I'll always be your mother, and I love you."

He blinked several times. *What was he keeping from her?* Now wasn't the time to press him, but one thing was for sure, she'd be praying for him. He shrugged. "I love you, too, Mum. I hope you'll be happy."

She smiled at him, the strong scent of his vanilla-rum cologne enveloping her. He filled out his shirt with muscles she'd never seen before. *Why hadn't she noticed?* He was such a good-looking man, so like his father. She gulped as the memory of Greg flitted across her mind. She and Bruce had talked at length about how they felt about their first loves and had accepted that his wife and her husband would always be there in their memories and hearts. Where they should be. She smiled again and rubbed Simon's arms. "Thank you."

"Come on, Mum, let's get you married."

Wendy leaned forward and hugged him before linking her arm through his. She inhaled slowly and stepped onto the sand.

BRUCE STOOD under the gazebo and gazed at his beautiful Wendy as she walked toward him on Simon's arm, her face beaming. When she reached him, he took her hand, leaned forward and kissed her cheek. They shared a smile that made his insides tingle.

They faced the Fijian minister they'd engaged to conduct the ceremony. They'd spoken with Joseph by phone and Skype on several occasions and were comfortable with his manner and understanding of their situation.

Wearing a traditional sulu, or skirt, and a floral short-sleeved shirt, he smiled broadly, flashing white teeth, and then officially welcomed them and their families. "Such a special occasion. The joining of two hearts and lives in holy matrimony, in this most beautiful of places. Let us begin." He paused, and smiled at Wendy and Bruce again addressing the family.

"Dearly Beloved, we are gathered here in the sight of God, and in the presence of these witnesses, to join together this man and woman in holy matrimony, an honorable estate, instituted of God, signifying the mystical union that exists between Christ and His Church. This holy estate Christ adorned with His presence and first miracle in Cana of Galilee, and St. Paul commended as being honorable among men. It is, therefore, not to be entered into lightly, but reverently, discreetly, and in the fear of God. Into this holy estate, Bruce and Wendy now come to be joined."

Bruce glanced at Wendy and grinned. Her hair ruffled in the light breeze, and she looked the epitome of beauty. Soon after, as he vowed to love and cherish her for the rest of his life, he thanked God once again for bringing her into his life.

When the minister pronounced them man and wife, he gazed into her eyes before kissing her for the first time as her husband. How he wanted this moment to last, but they had the rest of their lives together, so he just kissed her lightly. When their gazes connected and held, the genuine love in her eyes was more than he could ever have imagined or hoped for.

After sharing a light lunch with their families, Bruce and Wendy stepped onto the jetty and the luxury catamaran they'd hired for their first night together. They planned to spend the rest of the week with their families at the resort, but wanted one night alone.

That night, dining on a fresh seafood feast, the sky turned a brilliant orange as the sun set slowly over the sparkling sea. The gentle sound of water lapping against the hulls mingled with romantic music playing from the sound system inside the luxury boat. It was such a special night, one that he'd treasure forever.

As they approached the jetty the following day, a number of smaller catamarans were out on the water in front of the resort. Bruce smiled when he realized that Aiden and Paige were on one of them. He chuckled as he slipped his arm around his wife's shoulder. "An odd couple, but you never know." He laughed as he popped a kiss on Wendy's cheek. "Stranger things have been known to happen."

She chuckled. "Like you and me?"

"I didn't say that."

"You didn't have to." She wound her arms around his waist and lifted her face for a kiss. "I love you, Bruce McCarthy."

He stroked her hair gently and brushed his lips against hers. "And I love you right back, Mrs. McCarthy." Who would have thought his life would change so completely in such a short time? But he wouldn't have it any other way. This Texan cowboy loved his Aussie gal with his whole heart. When she slipped her hands around his neck and pressed her lips to his, Bruce's entire body responded.

WENDY PALMED HIS CHEEK. Who would have imagined she'd

have to suffer great loss only to find true love again? This was her destiny. Life was a road map to discovery, and her Texan cowboy was a treasure more precious than gold.

"*Give thanks to the Lord, for He is good; His love endures forever.*" Psalm 118:1

NOTE FROM THE AUTHOR

I hope you enjoyed "A Time to Treasure." Wendy and Bruce's story continues in "A Time to Care", coming soon! (I promise!)

To make sure you don't miss it, and to be notified of all my new releases, join Juliette's Readers' list. You'll also receive a free thank-you copy of "Hank and Sarah - A Love Story", a clean love story with God at the center. https://www.juliette-duncan.com/subscribe/

Enjoyed "A Time to Treasure"? You can make a big difference. Help other people find this book by writing a review and telling them why you liked it. Honest reviews of my books help bring them to the attention of other readers just like yourself, and I'd be very grateful if you could spare just five minutes to leave a review (it can be as short as you like) on the book's Amazon page.

Oh, and keep reading for a bonus chapter of "Tender Love". If you enjoyed "A Time to Treasure", I'm sure you'll also enjoy this one too.

Blessings,

Juliette

Chapter 1
Brisbane, Australia

EARLY MORNING SUNSHINE streamed through the white lace curtains of Tessa Scott's pocket-sized bedroom, but inside her heart, it rained. Nearly three months had passed since she had formally ended her relationship with Michael Urbane, and although she firmly believed it had been the right thing to do, pain still squeezed her heart whenever she thought of him.

Some days were easier than others, but the past two days had been especially hard. Yesterday had been Michael's birthday. How tempted she'd been to call him and at least wish him 'happy birthday'. Last year she'd surprised him with a day trip snorkelling on Moreton Island. They'd had so much fun—they always did, and the very memory of that wonderfully happy, sun-filled day only made it worse. She shouldn't let her mind go there, but she couldn't help it, and images of their day snorkelling amongst the coral and the myriads of brightly coloured fish played over and over in her mind.

Burying her head in her pillow, Tessa sobbed silent tears. It hurt so badly. If only the accident at his work hadn't happened. *Or he hadn't lied about the drugs.* She inhaled deeply as a sob escaped, sending another wave of sadness through her body. *Why couldn't she let go?* Maybe she should give him another chance? *But it would never be the same.* She knew that. Their adventure had died, and she needed to accept it.

A soft knock on the door interrupted her thoughts. The gentle but firm voice of her housemate, Stephanie, sounded on the other side. "Tess, you need to get up."

Tessa buried her head deeper in the pillows.

The door creaked open and Stephanie tip-toed in, placing a cup of spiced chai tea on Tessa's nightstand. The aromatic mixture of cardamom, cinnamon, ginger and other herbs filled the room, tickling her nose. Steph knew the trick to getting her up.

She gave in and raised her head. "What time is it?"

"Time to get up, that's what." Dressed in a smart business suit, Stephanie placed her hands on her hips and studied Tessa with an air of disapproval. "Don't tell me you've been crying over Michael again?"

Tessa sat up and took a sip of tea before meeting her friend's gaze. "Just thinking about him, that's all."

Stephanie shook her head and let out a frustrated sigh. "I know you're grieving, but it's been months since you broke up. Come on. Get out of bed and get ready for work. Your boss called and said she'd place you on unpaid leave if you call in sick one more time. I was tempted to tell her you weren't even sick."

"But I have been sick." Tessa leaned back against her bedhead and bit her lip, forcing herself not to cry in front of Stephanie.

"I know." Sitting on the edge of the bed, Stephanie took hold of Tessa's free hand. "It's hard to let go, especially having been together for so long. But breaking up was the only option. You know that."

"But maybe I was too hard on him." Tessa grabbed a tissue and wiped her eyes. "Those drugs changed him, Steph. He wasn't himself."

"I know. But you did try to help him. For months. I watched you slowly being torn apart. The truth is, you can't help someone who doesn't want to be helped." Stephanie squeezed her hand. "You can't help someone who lies to you about their addiction, even if it is to prescription drugs. *And he stole from you.* You need honesty in your relationship, and Michael wasn't willing to give that to you. You did the right thing. You're better off without him."

"It's just hard not knowing where he is or how he's doing." Tessa glanced at the photo of him still sitting on her dresser. "It's hard being single again. I feel …" She paused and searched for the right word, as the ache in her chest grew. "Lonely."

"You poor thing." Stephanie leaned forward and hugged her tightly. "I'm here for you, Tess. And so's God, you know that. I understand you feel bad about this whole situation, but God's with you, and He'll help you through it. And you never know what, or who, He might have in store for you!" She gently brushed the stray hair from Tessa's face and gave her another hug.

Tessa nodded reluctantly. Steph was right. She'd made the right decision and knew that God would be with her and would help her through it, but translating that knowledge to her heart was another matter altogether.

"Come on kiddo, breakfast's ready. Let's get you up, dressed, and off to work."

TESSA SLID out of bed as Stephanie retreated to the kitchen. As she swallowed down the rest of her tea, Michael's photo caught her attention once again. Grey eyes with a hint of blue in a tanned, chiselled face stared out at her, tugging at her heart-strings. She picked up the photo and flopped back onto her bed, gazing at the face that was so familiar. This torture had to end. She traced the outline of his face with her finger before hugging the photo to her chest. Closing her eyes, she squeezed back hot tears. This was it. The end.

"God, please help me get through this day." Her body shuddered as she gulped down unbidden sobs. *"I'm sorry it's taken so long, but I'm ready to let go. Please help me."* Tears streamed down her face as she hugged the photo tightly one last time before she opened the bottom drawer of her dresser and stuffed the photo under the pile of chunky knit sweaters she rarely wore.

Time to move on, and with God's help, she would.

Find all of Juliette Duncan's books on her website:
www.julietteduncan.com/library

A Time for Everything Series

A Time For Everything Series is a series of contemporary Christian romance novels set in Sydney, Australia, and Texas, USA. If you like real-life characters, faith-filled families, and friendships that become something more, then you'll love Juliette Duncan's inspirational second-chance romance.

A Time to Care

They've tied the knot, but will their love last the distance?

Wendy didn't expect to find love again after losing her beloved husband of over 30 years to a heart attack, but after being swept off her feet by a silver-haired Texan cowboy she met in a Dublin hotel, their relationship bloomed, and she agreed to marry him.

Now, Wendy couldn't be more content as she and Bruce settle into married life in her harbourside home in Sydney.

Bruce is besotted with his new wife and is adjusting well to life in the city, although he secretly hankers for land, horses and open spaces.

When Paige, Wendy's youngest daughter, announces she's pregnant and doesn't know who the father is, as loving Christian parents, Wendy and Bruce take her in and care for her, but she's rebellious and angry, and threatens to disrupt their peaceful life.

Is their love strong enough to survive this unexpected intrusion?

Billionaires with Heart Christian Romance Series

Her Kind-Hearted Billionaire

A reluctant billionaire, a grieving young woman, and the trip that changes their lives forever...

Her Generous Billionaire

A grieving billionaire, a solo mother, and a woman determined to sabotage their relationship...

Her Disgraced Billionaire

A messed up billionaire who lands in jail, a nurse who throws a challenge he can't refuse...

"The Billionaires with Heart Christian Romance Series" is a series

of stand-alone books that are both God honoring and
entertaining. Get your copy now,

enjoy and be blessed!

The True Love Series

Set in Australia, what starts out as simple love story grows into a
family saga, including a dad battling bouts of depression and guilt, an
ex-wife with issues of her own, and a young step-mum trying to
mother a teenager who's confused and hurting. Through it all, a love
story is woven. A love story between a caring God and His precious
children as He gently draws them to Himself and walks with them
through the trials and joys of life.

"A beautiful Christian story. I enjoyed all of the books in this series.
They all brought out Christian concepts of faith in action."

"Wonderful set of books. Weaving the books from story to story.
Family living, God, & learning to trust Him with all their hearts."

The Precious Love Series

The Precious Love Series continues the story of Ben, Tessa and Jayden from the The True Love Series, although each book can be read on its own. All of the books in this series will warm your heart and draw you closer to the God who loves and cherishes you without condition.

"I loved all the books by Juliette, but those about Jaydon and Angie's stories are my favorites...can't wait for the next one..."

"Juliette Duncan has earned my highest respect as a Christian romance writer. She continues to write such touching stories about real life and the tragedies, turmoils, and joys that happen while we are living. The words that she uses to write about her characters relationships with God can only come from someone that has had a very close & special with her Lord and Savior herself. I have read all of her books and if you are a reader of Christian fiction books I would highly recommend her books." Vicki

The Shadows Series

An inspirational romance, a story of passion and love, and of God's inexplicable desire to free people from pasts that haunt them so they can live a life full of His peace, love and forgiveness, regardless of the circumstances.

Book 1, *"Lingering Shadows"* is set in England, and follows the story of Lizzy, a headstrong, impulsive young lady from a privileged background, and Daniel, a roguish Irishman who sweeps her off her feet. But can Lizzy leave the shadows of her past behind and give Daniel the love he deserves, and will Daniel find freedom and release in God?

Hank and Sarah - A Love Story, *the Prequel to "The Madeleine Richards Series" is a FREE thank you gift for joining my mailing list. You'll also be the first to hear about my next books and get exclusive sneak previews. Get your free copy at www. julietteduncan.com/subscribe*

The Madeleine Richards Series

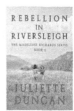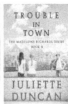

Although the 3 book series is intended mainly for pre-teen/ Middle Grade girls, it's been read and enjoyed by people of all ages.

"Juliette has a fabulous way of bringing her characters to life. Maddy is at typical teenager with authentic views and actions that truly make it feel like you are feeling her pain and angst. You want to enter into her situation and make everything better. Mom and soon to be dad respond to her with love and gentle persuasion while maintaining their faith and trust in Jesus, whom they know, will give them wisdom as they continue on their lives journey. Appropriate for teenage readers but any age can enjoy." Amazon Reader

The Potter's House Books...stories of hope, redemption, and second chances. Find out more here:

http://pottershousebooks.com/our-books/

The Homecoming

Kayla McCormack is a famous pop-star, but her life is a mess. Dane Carmichael has a disability, but he has a heart for God. He had a crush on her at school, but she doesn't remember him. His simple faith and life fascinate her, But can she surrender her life of fame and fortune to find true love?

Unchained

Imprisoned by greed – redeemed by love

Sally Richardson has it all. A devout, hard-working, well-respected husband, two great kids, a beautiful home, wonderful friends. Her life is perfect. Until it isn't.

When Brad Richardson, accountant, business owner, and respected church member, is sentenced to five years in jail, Sally is shell-shocked. How had she not known about her husband's fraudulent activity? And how, as an upstanding member of their tight-knit community, did he ever think he'd get away with it? He's defrauded clients, friends, and fellow church members. She doubts she can ever trust him again.

Locked up with murderers and armed robbers, Brad knows that the only way to survive his incarceration is to seek God with all his heart - something he should have done years ago. But how does he convince his family that his remorse is genuine? Will they ever forgive him?

He's failed them. But most of all, he's failed God. His poor decisions have ruined this once perfect family.

They've lost everything they once held dear. Will they lose each other as well?

~

Blessings of Love

She's going on mission to help others. He's going to win her heart.

Skye Matthews, bright, bubbly and a committed social work major, is the pastor's daughter. She's in love with Scott Anderson, the most eligible bachelor, not just at church, but in the entire town.

Scott lavishes her with flowers and jewellery and treats her like a lady, and Skye has no doubt that life with him would be amazing. And yet, sometimes, she can't help but feel he isn't committed enough. Not to her, but to God.

She knows how important Scott's work is to him, but she has a niggling feeling that he isn't prioritising his faith, and that concerns her. If only he'd join her on the mission trip to Burkina Faso...

Scott Anderson, a smart, handsome civil engineering graduate, has just received the promotion he's been working for for months. At age twenty-four, he's the youngest employee to ever hold a position of this calibre, and he's pumped.

Scott has been dating Skye long enough to know that she's 'the one', but just when he's about to propose, she asks him to go on mission with her. His plans of marrying her are thrown to the wind.

Can he jeopardise his career to go somewhere he's never heard of, to work amongst people he'd normally ignore?

If it's the only way to get a ring on Skye's finger, he might just risk it...

And can Skye's faith last the distance when she's confronted with a truth she never expected?

Stand Alone Christian Romantic Suspense

Leave Before He Kills You

When his face grew angry, I knew he could murder...

That face drove me and my three young daughters to flee across Australia.

I doubted he'd ever touch the girls, but if I wanted to live and see them grow, I had to do something.

The plan my friend had proposed was daring and bold, but it also gave me hope.

My heart thumped. What if he followed?

Radical, honest and real, this Christian romantic suspense is one woman's journey to freedom you won't put down...get your copy and read it now.

ABOUT THE AUTHOR

Juliette Duncan is a Christian fiction author, passionate about writing stories that will touch her readers' hearts and make a difference in their lives. Although a trained school teacher, Juliette spent many years working alongside her husband in their own business, but is now relishing the opportunity to follow her passion for writing stories she herself would love to read. Based in Brisbane, Australia, Juliette and her husband have five adult children, seven grandchildren, and an elderly long haired dachshund. Apart from writing, Juliette loves exploring the great world we live in, and has travelled extensively, both within Australia and overseas. She also enjoys social dancing and eating out.

Connect with Juliette:

Email: juliette@julietteduncan.com

Website: www.julietteduncan.com

Facebook: www.facebook.com/JulietteDuncanAuthor

Twitter: https://twitter.com/Juliette_Duncan

Made in the USA
Monee, IL
12 August 2021